Eden

Olympia Vernon

Eden

Grove Press
New York

Published simultaneously in Canada
Printed in the United States of America

FIRST EDITION

Library of Congress Cataloging-in-Publication Data
Vernon, Olympia
    Eden / Olympia Vernon.—1st ed.
      p. cm.
    ISBN 0-8021-1728-7
    1. African American teenage girls—Fiction.   2. African American families—
Fiction.   3. African American women—Fiction.   4. Rural families—
Fiction.   5. Mississippi—Fiction.   I. Title.
PS3622.E75 E34 2003
813'.6—dc21   2002033863

Grove Press
841 Broadway
New York, NY 10003

03 04 05 06   10 9 8 7 6 5 4 3 2 1

To God, the angels for rousing me out of my sleep to write this novel, and the children of Independence Middle School for sharing the happiness within them, during moments when my heart was in a great flood.

Do you think you shall enter the garden of bliss without such trials as those who have passed before you?

—The Koran

Eden

chapter
one

One Sunday morning, during Bible study, I took a tube of Aunt Pip's fire-engine-red lipstick and drew a naked lady over the first page of Genesis. Her chest was as flat as a man's, her face blank and clear. The language was loose around me, as I remember the sound of Mama's voice and the question that came along with it, the one that counted: "Don't you know that blood and milk is the same?" She shook me between her words. "They can't sit out long before the world get wind o' 'em and the next thing you know they caught in the tubes and the devil come out and you end up titty sick; 'cause he be red, red like this here mess you done made."

The clouds were dark. I sensed that it would, indeed, rain because of the birthmark on Mama's forehead. It was a long, winding, tornado-shaped birthmark below her widow's peak. It was a red stirring of her soul. She always pulled it back before the storm to witness its color change in the mirror.

"I keep at you, Maddy," said Mama as she pulled a bucket of collard greens between her legs and took a small batch of them between her thick, round fingers. "Ain't nothing going to waste now. It's all a part of itself."

She worked the garden behind our house barefoot. I walked behind her sometimes to measure the weight of my bones in her footprints: the imperfect arch, the heel curved into the marrow of an athlete's laughter—where the side of his face is flat at the jawbone like an old habit, wide, invisible. Every now and then, she'd laugh and hold her chest and tell me that my hips were as clear as *Jesus'*.

"Yes, ma'am," I said.

Grandma passed away years earlier. Sometimes a gust of wind drifted through the screen door and I could smell her wrinkled, pale body when she had taken off her panties to draw a bath. And the green lizard in her hands that she'd kept in a mason jar for hours at a time because it was the closest thing to the earth and the people in it.

The house was warm. I once heard that whatever god a person believed in, that god would look just like him. But something was wrong with the gods in my house. None of them looked like me. They were blue-eyed and dirty-blond. Upright, narrow-jawed. Those same gods I saw during communion where there was no wine or cracker if I didn't first praise Him and believe that He gave me life. I did until I went to take Miss Hattie Mae, the neighbor, a bowl of sugar for her potato pone. There I saw, for the first time, a black God.

Miss Hattie Mae, a widow who never let anyone inside her house, walked forward with the bones in her hands covered by a thin layer of ointment. "It's the arthritis," she said. "Put the sugar on the kitchen table." I saw Him there behind her, His arms on the cross, His orange eyes. Miss Hattie Mae was a thin, cautious woman with the scent of bananas trailing a pattern throughout her house. "Go on," she said as the fumes of the ointment made my eyes watery. "Go."

Mama wiped the sweat from her forehead with a table napkin. It was white with blue horizontal lines going through it. She walked over to the kitchen sink and paused. All that flesh to haul around weighed down on her. She hated being a big woman, being out of breath all the time with that loose fat draining all of her energy. "Reckon your Daddy be home soon?"

"Yes, ma'am," I said. "He's been out since Thursday."

Now it was Saturday. He had gone to Morgan City, Louisiana, to slaughter a hog that he'd fattened. Everyone in town knew that it didn't take three days to kill no hog. He lied. He told Mama that it took so long because he and the boys had to bless the meat.

"I'm wishing we had the killing," said Mama. "It'll go right nice with these here collards."

She had traded her life for him. I had seen her in pictures at sixteen before the fatness of her body swallowed her. One arm wrapped around Daddy's throat from behind, the laughter on her face as light and delicate as lint on a child's clothes. Because her belly was flat then and there were no babies to swell her. Because she loved him the way he was and had taught him the vocabulary of the liquor labels, the clear from the dark. She had fallen in love with an illiterate man, her fingers now mocking the shapes of caterpillars from hard work, a maid's work. Because she knew that there would be times when she'd drop him off at Mr. Sandifer's, his boss at the scrap yard, and his feet would never touch the ground.

"I smell Grandma," I said.

Again she paused, looking out at the empty hog pen, remembering the night that Grandma chopped off Daddy's arm with the ax because he smelled like thievery. Thievery to Grandma was anything less than Mama and nothing greater. The blood stayed in the house for three days. She made him step over it every morning on his way to work. It seemed like forever before the smell of blood and maggots cleared the air.

"I smell her too," she said.

There fell a moment of silence between us.

Mama looked at her hands and moaned. She was made of a glass vase. Her throat was sharp and fragile, her lips clear, smooth. She picked up a porcelain paragraph filled with the words of *Jesus*. Grandma always said that an object in a woman's hands was the way she chose to lose a headache. She said this, that women who did not use their words caught a headache of the mind and spirit. If a woman was too weak to use her voice, her vocabulary got trapped in her temples and formed a blood clot. And with this came the disaster of silence.

She was thinking of Aunt Pip now, the evening the church folk came by for a cold drink of lemonade and a helping of potato pone, the moment she noticed that Daddy and Aunt Pip were missing and found an empty bottle of whiskey on the kitchen table. She was a woman with a need for moving things in her life. My father was her balance. He was her baptism. Before long, she was turning away from the voices, the gravity of gossip in the front yard, only to find Daddy's fingers going up the hole in Aunt Pip's vagina. She said nothing. She knew the difference between a man wanting her and needing her. What could she have done? She was a maid for damn near every white man in Pyke County. And men loved Aunt Pip. She knew how to walk with her shoulders up. She was a thin woman, useful. Mama thought of many things: the time she caught Daddy at the pool hall with that Jefferson girl, when she broke his collarbone in two places and no doctor would fix it because of his reputation, Jesus. She did nothing. Just stood there in the backyard for hours holding the tube of fire-engine-red lipstick that Aunt Pip had left behind, crying silently.

Eventually, she spoke. Daddy had been at a cockfight all evening. And for some reason, he forgot that Mama was a woman who didn't forget things. He thought her words would stay pinned up in her head. But I knew that she didn't forget things: iron the sheets, stretch the towels out on the line, stop by the post office, remember the numbers. Lord, have mercy. Don't ever forget the numbers. Never get a white man's mail mixed up with a Negro's. No man's numbers were ever the same. His numbers were his life. And do those white man's favors and remember to use that weariness against your sister. Remember to curse her out for sleeping with your husband. And don't ever listen. Curse until your lungs close in on you and shut you down.

I could still hear the words, the cursing Mama put on Aunt Pip. She didn't know words like that. Not Mama. She was a quiet woman, useful to the world. She didn't curse. I told myself a lot of things. A lot of wrong, but rational things to keep from killing them like the dead bird that I'd found in the road: the eyes covered by a white film, the dark pupil underneath, circular. On that particular day, the day Mama chose to use her voice, I brought the dead bird home and threw it against my bedroom mirror until the eyes closed and it knew nothing else of the world. It did not stop the sound of the voices; my grandma held her chest and stretched her arms out to Mama and Aunt Pip, ordering them to stop hollering inside her house. The sound of the screen door slamming and the flies buzzed over a piece of sliced watermelon on the front porch. Grandma clenched her blouse and mumbled, "Y'all gone kill me." A couple of days later, Aunt Pip sent me in the house to get Grandma. But I told her that she was too sick to get up. In her place, she had given me a green garden lizard to put inside Aunt Pip's hands, saying: "This is my home. I left my heart here."

Yeah, it was a man who had separated Mama and Aunt Pip. Daddy had met them both at the pool hall. He was a young, well-built man with an odor on him. I'd heard men from Morgan City ask him about his fingers, if the smell of pussy was still on them. They said that he'd push his fingers so far up a woman's stomach that he pulled the cord out. And when she went to pee, blood came from her. He had used his fingers to embarrass. This gave him power.

"The rain'll be here the reckon," said Mama. "Get the clothes off the line."

The spring air floated upward. My fingers were wrinkled from the bucket of water, the collard greens. I missed the hog. I liked having something active around. The night before Daddy took the hog to Morgan City, I walked over to the gate and opened it. The hog licked her fur in the corner of the pen. She was afraid of me that night. Something kept her there. I opened the gate to free her. She didn't move. "The men will kill you," I said. "They will eat you and take your fur." I hadn't used my fingers enough to touch her. I was human. She didn't trust human hands. Humans killed. They killed and ate what they killed. She felt that as I stared into her eyes and found myself there dying to find the part of me that belonged, that wasn't green and afraid. I saw love in her eyes. She knew how to love. A hog who ate and loved what loved her. I slowly walked backward to find her so afraid of freedom that when the gate was completely open, she found herself cradled inside the sharpest corner of the pen, licking her private parts.

Grandma had walked clean out the back door with Daddy's arm in her hand. I remember the commotion, the loud voices, Daddy telling Grandma to shut her old ass up. Phrases, secrets that went right over my head. Mama crying for Grandma to stop before her heart stopped working. "I chop my own wood," said Grandma. "I've always chopped my own wood!" She was a strong woman. She hated the weak. "It's all right if you can't see my heart from the inside," she said. "My child is my business. It's her heart they stare at when you can't pay the bills." She called on God. "Her heart is on the outside now. You took her pride. It's not even her pain no more. Now she belong to the world." She yelled those words over and over again as if she'd rehearsed them. Daddy said something. Next thing I know, Daddy's screaming and there's a pool of blood on the floor.

Everything was so blurry. Mama hanging over Daddy's chest and pushing me against the walls. Her saying that Daddy's life was missing. Grandma took his life. The backyard covered in a blanket of blue. The eye sees most when it's not looking, as I witnessed the shape of my grandma's crawling hair marching out to the hog pen with Daddy's arm in her hand. She didn't just turn around. She stayed there awhile with Daddy's arm in one hand and an ax in the other. Daddy's arm: the radius of a complete body, the portion of a man that every man needed, his trouble, a six-sided dice throw against the wall, an acoustic guitar's whine, half his life. Grandma dumped it into the trough. I was sure of it. That's why my daddy hated that hog so much. After that night, he fed it anything he could get his hands on. That hog had eaten his arm, his manhood, his work. Yeah, he fattened that hog up real nice before he drove all the way to Morgan City to kill it, because it had lived too close to his memory, so close to his house to have owned his house, owned him.

I gathered a load of sheets in my arms before going back into the house.

"Are they sour?" Mama asked.

I smelled them. "No, ma'am."

The rain came pouring down. I went to my room to listen to it, to become a part of my God, to leave behind the quiet silence between a mother and child who didn't know how to talk to each other, how to fully communicate about the dead, the cheating, the alcoholic father, the whispers in town about a sinful child with no respect for God's house, His rules.

I always had my encyclopedias. I hated history. If it hadn't been for that one subject, I would have been an honor student. I read everything. Paid more attention to Negroes than they had to themselves. I knew why that hog didn't come to me too. I read things about those white scientists and how people, animals, were conditioned to a sort of "used to" type of living. That hog was so used to being locked up that she didn't know how to move or break the rules. She lay there like that because she was used to being confined, eating slop. I mean she was so used to eating slop that my daddy's arm went right down her throat, fingers and all.

"I got a telegram today," said Mama. I folded my arms and leaned my head to one side as her shadow grew larger over the edge of my bed. Finally, she sat down. The pot on the stove was boiling over, full. "Pip's sick."

I heard that line over and over again in my head. That "Pip's sick" and there was something she wanted me to do about it, something I, a fourteen-year-old child, was supposed to do about it.

"Pack your things," she said. "You going to Commitment."

There was a nerve of electricity in her mouth, a tiny movement of activity riding the side of her jawbone as if a parasite had gotten trapped inside.

"What kind of sick?" I asked.

She went for the door again. Her shadow halted. She had not seen Aunt Pip since Grandma's funeral. Even then, they did not say one word to each other.

"Graveyard sick," she said.

Later that evening, we drove to the outskirts of Pyke County. Aunt Pip lived on Commitment Road with one other lady who didn't belong to any church for miles around. And she used her social security check to pay her bills. She, like Miss Hattie Mae, was a widow.

"Maddy," said Mama, pulling her Goodwill hat over to one side and giving me the eye in the rearview mirror. "Make sure that if you and Pip leave the house, you put on some underclothes. Never know what could happen these days."

There were tiny holes in the floor panel. When she drove, the dirt road underneath my feet reminded me of time and its passing. After Grandma died, the folks at the funeral home sent word that Mama needed to bring her some more comfortable shoes to be buried in. Only the oldest child was allowed to see the dead. Nobody else. The telegram said that Grandma's feet were swollen. I sat in that very seat, drawing the letters of my name on the windows, looking down at Grandma's shoes, hoping that she'd come alive in them. It was muddy that day. The sky didn't have a color in it.

"Yes, ma'am."

Two church members followed closely behind us in the rearview mirror. A woman in a white hat threw her hands up. Every so often, her husband, in his brown suit, would take one hand off the wheel and bring it to his forehead. The wife was holding a Bible up now. They were like Adam and Eve discussing sin. Whose voice mattered most I did not know. The husband, his face microscopic, lit a cigar.

The road was wet as leaves of thick, fat pine trees grazed the windshield. Mama slowed down, complaining about the car's hanging muffler. "Lawd," she said, "the only good your daddy give me was a nine-month-old seed."

"Even that doesn't count," I said.

She didn't understand me. We didn't understand each other. "What?" she said.

"Women hold babies for almost a year," I said. "And when it comes out, they have to start all over again." My nose itched. "That's not fair."

"Well," said Mama, "some babies come out early. You was so small I thought the flies would eat you alive."

"But Ma," I said, "almost a year?"

"That's the way God made us, Maddy."

"I'm actually fifteen," I said. "A year older than I'm supposed to be."

"You lose something with age," she said, slowing down to escape a large hole in the road. She didn't know anything else. She knew only what she lost. "Don't ask for more than you need if you can help it."

She watched as the cows hovered over blocks of salt in the pasture, the glass vase in her throat vibrating. "No other part will ever matter as much as the outside part," she said. The electricity was in her hands now; she nursed it and rubbed it inside her hands like a dead bird with dead eyes. "What's going on?" she said.

One of Pillar's cows blocked the road. She blew the horn, but the cow didn't move. A big, grown cow with one of Pillar's tags clamped on her. Something so slow and patient belonged to a troubled man. A backslider like Pillar.

"Ma," I said, "roll your window down."

"What for?"

"So I can touch her," I said.

"Are you out o' your mind, Maddy?" Mama turned around and pulled my hair down. "Grease this stuff up real good before you go to bed. And don't forget to take the rubber bands out. They'll give you a headache something wicked."

"She won't hurt me," I said.

The sound of my voice irritated her. I embarrassed her in front of the church. Everybody knew that her sister had slept with her husband. They knew who the fire-engine-red lipstick belonged to. "The devil sent you," said one of the ushers. I'll never forget the feeling of her hands on my wrists; it was like a single leaded bullet trapped beneath the wings of a dead bird, mechanical.

"Cows hate red," said Mama. "You know that."

"But I'm not wearing red, Ma."

She pretended not to notice me. She was a Christian woman. The devil tried her. He wanted her to mess up that good religion of hers and come to him. He wanted her but sent for Aunt Pip.

"I wonder if Mr. Clyde knows that one o' his cows is out," Mama said. "I wouldn't want nobody to have no accident out here. Something that big could kill."

The cow didn't budge. A gnat flew around her ass, followed by other gnats that clung to the brown patches of her skin; her nipples sagged. "Come on now," said Mama as she pressed down on the horn. Mama grew distant. She didn't have to tell me. Aunt Pip's milk had turned sour. A lump was growing inside of her, a lump the size of a headache.

I had seen it in the encyclopedias that Mama had bought for me, how the milk was born to the mammal of a woman, running up through the tubes of her stomach, ending up in her breasts, forming a clot. The encyclopedias had been my language, the language that I spoke of only inside my head.

"Lawd, have mercy," said Mama, putting pressure on the horn.

The husband and wife were somewhere on the connecting roads now, talking about the naked lady, how well the fur between her legs was drawn but that her breasts were missing. I wasn't a normal fourteen-year-old. Something was wrong with me, let them tell it. A woman with no breasts? The sound of the wife and husband's motor went ricocheting through the trees, spreading gossip from house to house like a line of smoke from a sinner's pipe.

We turned down the road to Aunt Pip's place. The widow across the way had every light on in her house, it seemed. The shingles were lapped, one on top of the other, like sleeping men of old age. It was rare that a house had so much light on a rainy day. Negroes mostly found a safe spot, a bedroom, and went to sleep until the storm was over. But not her. As we passed her house, I turned my head and watched the curtains slowly open; her large index finger emerged.

"Behave yourself," said Mama. "I don't want nobody telling me you didn't mind."

She dropped me off in front of Aunt Pip's place and told me to go inside. "Take care," she said as she drove down the road with the fat of her arm hanging from the driver's side.

I was at the house where the dying lived. There was a sort of cold gray energy around me. The slow wind at my shoulders was loose, tiring.

The door opened. Aunt Pip stepped on the front porch, her face tender and dry around the edges. The bones in her neck were sharp, visible. A fragile woman with the skeletal framework of her body moving forward as if the metamorphosis of the hour kept her lungs weak and without breath.

"You just gone stand there, Maddy?" she asked. "Come on in."

She was the beginning.

"Mama would've come in," I said, stepping inside the house, "but she had a pot of greens on the stove."

The room was intimate, rectangular. Everything seemed motionless: the mute pattern of a record player, the dust of paragraphs written on solid objects, a porcelain doll with her mouth open. Inanimate things that fit inside the tiny room because a woman needed something to talk to. She had positioned them in an order of speech, as if this were her room of solitude where her voice could match perfectly the placing of paragraphs and record players and dolls.

A strong odor of VapoRub came through. The couch where Big Mama had died after getting her legs amputated was still there. Big Mama was an independent woman. She couldn't deal with her legs being gone and having people around the place pushing her around and sniffing her panties to see if she had peed on herself. A woman who, like her daughter, was used to chopping her own wood and stacking it against the side of the house. That's what happened to her. Having to be dependent on mankind killed her.

The house was warm. The dark clouds were fading behind the magnolias. The earth had become pregnant with silence, a few birds flying through the trees, the occasional barking of a dog in the distance. There was a fireplace in the middle of the rectangular room. Ashes had mounted up inside it. It was the first sign of loneliness, detachment. I looked around at the photos. One in particular: a black-and-white photograph of two small children. The bright hue of the cotton field smothered the light in their eyes. A coldness that I couldn't pinpoint.

"Turnips or collards?" asked Aunt Pip; her voice sounded distant, battered.

"Ma'am?"

"What grade of greens? Turnips or collards?"

"Oh, collards."

We had been close once; she had given me the drag of my first cigarette, taught me things about my period and boys. And how to tell the difference between shit and diarrhea when it came to a man. "Shit," she'd say, "is what they get stuck into, but diarrhea is when one lie turns into another one and they all become one great big lie. Trust me, child. All men lie. In one way or another, they all do."

"One minute," said Aunt Pip.

The bed next to the fireplace was covered in ants. I killed them with my fingers and waited for Aunt Pip to emerge from the connecting room. Big Mama's curtains were still there. The rods were not made of aluminum or iron. They'd been made from the twigs of a magnolia. Big Mama loved magnolias. Once the flowers wilted, she took them inside the house and stripped the branches bare. She would show me the curves. "This is a woman's body," she'd say. "I'm putting her clothes on. She will live here with me until I'm gone. She will never leave me." I felt her spirit in the house as I ran my fingers across the dead ants. I don't know why I killed them. One by one, I put them in the windowsill, aligning them as if they were crushed powder or bone.

I ran my fingers over the shape of Aunt Pip's body; a pattern was deeply molded into the bedspread. The long arms. The covey hole from the weight of her elbow. A small, distinct hole that showed clearly where her pain sank down into her elbows at night. Beside the bed sat a Styrofoam bust of a lady's head and shoulders covered with a pink scarf. Rainwater came down on it; the roof had a hole in it.

"Make yourself comfortable," she said.

I was growing older. At fourteen, I had never kissed a boy or let him stroke my pubic hair. I had seen a penis only when I walked in on my daddy using the john. I knew very little about myself. I

knew little because there were things I was not supposed to do as
a Negro child, questions I was not supposed to ask. I knew one thing
and wore it alone. I knew to act Negro when other Negroes were
around, not to talk about the bones I studied in the encyclopedia,
the different species of animals, the words that Negroes in Pyke
County never used. I was not to know why my ideas, my thoughts,
my body were often too much for me. Or why I came home from
school one day with a dead bird inside my hands, why I killed it to
save it.

"Come see," said Aunt Pip.

The rectangular room was blocked off by a thin paisley-printed
sheet. It bore an odor that was strange, haunting.

"Do you reckon it's on wrong?" asked Aunt Pip.

Aunt Pip stood before me with her gown pulled down to her
waist, her bra exposed. I looked first at her face, the light eyebrows,
the chiseled nose above her lips, how the yellow eyes turned away,
focusing on a distant thing with no name. Down toward the neck,
the throat, the aisle of bones in the middle of her chest. And there
it was, a scar where her left breast used to be, running across her
skin in the shape of a glass-trapped lizard, quiet, disturbed.

She walked over to the king-size bed and sat down. It angered
me that she didn't have the energy to do it herself. She wasn't this
way. What happened to her strength? Where were her lovers?
Where was Mama? They all sent me: Mama, the town, my father,
Jesus.

"I'll help you," I said.

My hands trembled. I was afraid of the disease, the cancer. The
heat from her body was warm. Willie Patterson, a boy whose parents died because his mama was breast-feeding him while driving,
was called retarded by the boys at school. And what of Aunt Pip?
If the boys had seen her now, she'd be another retarded Willie.

Retarded. A word I never looked up in the dictionary because it was worse than being called a nigger. A word with its own dysfunction, an ugly, bare-faced word that went straight from a child's mouth and into the cruel, nasty world that gave birth to it.

"Don't be ashamed," said Aunt Pip. "We got the same things."

I wanted to hate her for asking me to come around from the backside, to witness her body from the front where the lizard on her chest lay motionless; it was her life. Not mine.

"Yes, ma'am."

What happened to a woman with half her life? Where did it go? What did the doctors do with the breast after they took it away? Men talked about women with only one breast. One wasn't enough. Women needed two breasts. Because men needed flesh.

"Touch it," she said.

"No," I said, "I can't."

"Here," she said, with my hand in hers.

I touched where her left breast used to be, where the lizard lay half asleep, his stomach flat across the flesh, his tail frozen. And the other breast—the full one—as it sagged in the mirror; it was the head of a swan. It was warm like the blue-eyed Christ.

It was God.

"It's needed, child," she said. "You can't ignore change if it's teething."

Daddy took a chance with her because she was brave. Courage didn't live in Pyke County, Mississippi, if you were a woman. You got it the best way you knew how. Aunt Pip didn't take lessons. She hustled. She hustled so much that she could afford to let her sister's old man put his fingers up her vagina. The women in Pyke County didn't use their eyes. Like Mama, they used their hearts. Daddy was hip to that. Men gossiped about it. They killed other men for stealing their lady's eyes. Daddy was a drunk who grew tired of Mama and her God. The late nights bothered him. The times when he begged Mama to get off her knees and come to bed, make love to him for the man he was. Not the man he was not.

"This ain't misery, Maddy," Aunt Pip said. "We've got till Sunday and every other weekend until school is out. You have to do this. You have to because you want to. Otherwise, you're no good for me. I need somebody to be good for me."

She coughed from her lungs, holding on to me. Her bones were so light that I could have picked her up and carried her anywhere in the house she wanted to go. "It's the machines," she said. "Them doctors put my titty in the system."

Her bones were unencyclopedic. Yeah, I had seen the pictures of mammals and milk going up through the stomach. But nowhere had man put into image what happened to a woman's body after the milk in her breasts had spoiled.

This is the way that it was in the beginning. Aunt Pip had gotten caught in the tubes of my grandmother's stomach, and a midwife had to run and pull her out. And when she came to be, she was given to my great-grandmother to raise. Big Mama had been raped by a white man in the cornfields of Pyke County, Mississippi. She had known what it was to lift a baby's shoulders because her own had been lifted. She was given the duty of lifting Aunt Pip's shoulders because she knew that her daughter didn't have it in her to sleep with a lost baby, the smell of near death on her, reminding her of how close they had both come to dying, mortality.

Aunt Pip's scalp was naked. The veins sprouted into a small muscle underneath her scalp, as if someone had traced a route to California on there with the sharp lead of a no. 2 pencil. The world was a cruel place to be at death, especially when the town of your birth had condemned you into the shape of a harlot, unworthy of the hand of God to release you from the thing that diseased you.

"It's handling me, Maddy," she said with her head over the toilet, tears flowing. A thin line of saliva hung from the porcelain to her mouth. "Lawd, help me."

Her body was fragile. The bones felt like powder. To touch them was to bruise them. A tear formed on my inner eyelid. The water came up from the pit of my stomach through the cartilage of my entire body. And were it to slip from my eye and join hers, it would have caused her own to fill even more so with tears.

She vomited a stream of liquid. The saliva around her mouth was as I had seen in cattle, the mouth wide open to a position of uncertainty, the tongue coated white like the body of grease on a newborn baby.

A dog barked in the distance. The sound of its vocal cords was sharp, as if something had hit her. The bark turned into a cry that floated across the earth and landed on the surface of a distant thing.

Up high, the magnolia tree stood away from the window. The petals of alabaster flowers were beginning to sprout. The coming heat had rotted them into a limp brown state like the upper torso of an old woman reaching down to retrieve her husband's house slippers.

Aunt Pip wiped her mouth. "Jesus," she said.

When her hand landed on the porcelain, she noticed the veins of her wrists spreading up to her palm like a baywood tree. This is when the curiosity of her anatomy caused her to forget, in a childlike way, the existence of her crying. Her face was drawn downward, her mouth open.

"Look," she said. "I have a ditch in my bones."

At which point I felt the two tiny vertical bones of powder. They were underneath the baywood tree. She took my index finger and hard-pressed them. I ran it southward until I could no longer feel them. They had invisibly found themselves in a motion of blood and muscle going up to her elbow.

"No," she said, "this here." Between the powdered bones was a gap wide enough for a fingernail to run through it. I held her wrist in my hand and satisfied her.

"Yeah," I said, "I feel it."

I wanted to tell her the truth, not that I'd felt a ditch in her bones but what Daddy had told me when I was just nine years old. Nine was important. Three multiplied times three: the Father, the Son, and the Holy Spirit. Daddy gave me what he called "the reason why titties got so sick." He said that when he used to milk cattle, sometimes the mama cows would get so loud and heavy that you'd have thought the devil got clean inside of them. He said he'd go to squeezing their titties and they'd go to kicking and screaming until a hard lump came out of them. It was leftover milk that the calves didn't drink. It was wasted, spoiled and sour. It had hardened inside their titties and created a grown, painful lump of cancer.

An unexpected wind came through the bathroom window, causing one of the medicine bottles to fall from the exposed shelf. It rolled toward Aunt Pip's feet, across the wooden floor, rocking back and forth. She listened to the roaring of the pills inside a closed space. Her skin was dark from the therapy, the doctors being rough with her.

She touched her bald head and sighed, turning away from the settling pills. "My hair is gone," she said. "The doctors. They took my lady." She grabbed my clothes. "Is my hair gone, Maddy?" Her face fell downward toward the vomit that had coated the water like the yellow reflection of pee from a bladder. "Where my hair?"

Her insanity somehow pleased her. It belonged to her. As empty and burrowed as she had become, this was the only thing she was sure of, that she had a right to lose her mind because dementia was as certain as death.

"Somewhere naked," I said. "It'll grow again in another time."

She took these words and repeated them, looking back at the medicine bottle, at her reflection. "In my dreams," she said, "I sit between *Jesus'* legs, and he plait me into two."

I smiled, watching her hands leave her scalp. She took one finger and poked the vomit that lay restless on the spine of the toilet water. Her reflection rippled from the inside to the controlled edges of the porcelain. "Yeah," she said. "I get it back in another life."

I learned to fill her glass with hot water, as it caused the pain pills to dissolve quicker. When she went to undress herself, the other breast was still tattooed with circles where the doctors in Jackson had experimented on her. She said they put round Band-Aids there. They were connected to wires, thin wires that were hooked up to a machine.

She lay on the bed next to the open door, purring through the walls of the house like a baby after a nipple slips out of its mouth. She lay fetally positioned, her toes curled beneath her. The muscles in her legs carried a perfect arch, the calves hardening at her discomfort. I went to drape a wool blanket over her. "No," she said. "Leave me be."

At that moment, her eyes were fixed on the dead-end wall. She had covered her head with a pink scarf. She had not yet become used to lying on pillows with a naked scalp.

"Okay," I said.

What had the doctors done to her strength? It was as brutal as Samson to trust the thing that stole his power. I felt this way. Some part of her had trusted the doctors. One breast was gone without any experiments at all. The other she relied on hope, that God would put the miracle of His faith in a lighted machine, operable by a trained hand of medicine, that would free her from death.

I was sitting on the porch when midnight came down. The widow appeared through the darkness, holding a lantern and something else that I could not see. Her feet were heavy on the earth. Her body made its own noise, as if she was sure of the purpose of her steps, the way the moon hung over the magnolias. She went to the mailbox and put the thing in her hand inside and walked away.

"Appreciate it," I yelled.

My voice carried, but even this did not stop her, the lantern in her hand leading her back to the house where I'd first seen her finger emerge from the curtains. I brought the package inside: three tubes of fire-engine-red lipstick with a note that read: "Stay alive to enjoy this."

chapter
two

He told her he would kill her if she didn't open the door.

Daddy's drinking worsened. The thoughts set in. He was married to a woman whose mother took his manhood. He loved and hated Mama at the same time. Grandma always said that a drunk man told the truth. During that time when his head was no longer attached to his body, he didn't care about the world and how it judged him. He used his memory. He thought of all the things he couldn't say when he was sober and found the first victim to take it out on. A one-armed man didn't know shit about staying clean. His muscles, his rules, his lies had been established through his hands. He needed that missing arm for anger, to grab a woman's throat and strangle the Christ out of her.

"Open this door," he said as he stood outside the bedroom door and bitched to high heaven that he had had enough of God living in his house, sleeping with his wife, and tonight she would open the door or he would get his rifle, his double-gauge shotgun, and teach her to respect his house, his rules. "I mean it!"

"I'm not for it, Chevrolet," said Mama. "Not tonight."

God didn't live in his bedroom. Anything that came from God made my father angry. Where was God when he lost his manhood?

Where was He when Daddy needed a piece of Mama and couldn't get it? It hurt him to be mean to her. He didn't want to. I saw it in his eyes.

"Goddammit, Ann," he shouted. "You'd better open this door, if you know what's good for you."

He paced back and forth across the floorboards with his tall, narrow shadow bent at the shoulders. His rising arm hovered over his head, the Afro that he so proudly restored every morning with a wide-toothed comb. I was afraid to get up and close my door, to tell him that he couldn't come inside her because he had fucked up. She was a God-fearing woman, and he had fucked up.

"Get on away from here, Chevrolet." She winced. "You'd better kiss my ass if you know what's best."

She didn't mean it. He knew she didn't mean it. It happened every so often. She played the strong role and gave him the idea that she had an even thicker backbone than the whores he'd slept with. Everybody saw him with whores. Women who didn't love their kids as much as Mama loved me. Whores. Women with little or no Christ in their lives. But women just the same.

"Come on, now, baby," he said.

He worked hard all week. On Fridays, when Mama asked him where the money was, he told her that the guys on Factory took it. In other words, he spent every penny at the pool hall. Factory Road was less than half a mile from the house. Most of the people in Pyke County had died there: an endless list of drunks, petty thieves, hustlers. My daddy just hadn't had his time. God was not yet ready for him.

"Take heed," said Mama.

Although he hadn't hit her in a long time, she knew that if she'd opened the door right away, that lip of hers would be just as bloody and fat as the mamas of the kids at school.

"You hear me?" said Daddy as he kicked the face of the door until the wood resembled a grave digger's shovel. Chips of wood surfaced. He cursed and swung his fist until he grew tired, breathing heavily like he did the night he walked outside in the nude. The night Mama and I carried him inside the house before the neighbors woke up.

"God don't like ugly, Chevrolet," said Mama.

My bedroom door was open. I lay underneath the blanket and watched him; his nostrils were flaring. He paced the floor again and paused a second to look at the damage he'd done. He paced again before stopping to run his hand across the shovel. "He would if he lived in this motherfucker," he said.

"Quit now," said Mama.

Daddy tugged at his clothes. He didn't wear his clothes the same anymore. One of his shoulders was light. He was used to carrying more pride around with him. He started for the top button of his oxford. "Shit," he said. Mama had practiced with him for hours after his arm was cut off, just as she had with the liquor labels, teaching him how to undo his buttons by himself. Once he figured out what world a man of his condition belonged to, he perfected it. He walked his fingers down his shirt and unbuttoned the oxford.

"Chevrolet?" asked Mama.

The sound of worry was in her voice. He liked to get naked while drunk. A drunk man used his whiskey as an excuse to be yellow. He was a coward. His voice was inside his whiskey. It spoke for him and loved him. Never told him when he was wrong or that his child was right across the hall from him, watching him make a fool of himself.

"Answer me something," said Mama.

"All right," he said, with his hand nestled in his lap as if he had been holding a rabbit. "I'm loving me. You don't love me like I love me."

He was a child, a little boy with a body of missing fingers. Where was he? What place denied him the liberty of taking off his clothes? The anger inside him crawled into his missing fingers, where the liquor had stretched out the phantom. The spirit of his arm was somewhere inside his anxiety, scratching the hairs on his head.

"I do love you, Chevrolet," said Mama.

His penis hung over his balls as he pulled the long johns down to his knees. He wanted Mama to see his large dick. It was the only thing he could offer her. He let it go and knocked on the bedroom door with his face lying flat against the wooden surface.

"You don't want me," he said.

He cried in front of the door with that big dick in his hand. The bathroom light shone on his naked body. That nub hung from his shoulder like the arm of an octopus. In no time, he'd be whispering in her ear and holding his thing against her ass. She'd fuss a little and tell him to be quiet, to behave himself. Before she knew it, that long piece of Negro'd be sliding between her legs and Daddy'd be saying "Amen."

"Chevrolet," said Mama.

He lifted his head for a moment, his shadow weaving across the floor. He turned with his back to the door. The vivid money-green tattoo across his chest was carved with a baby pin and blue ink. He walked into the bathroom light and looked down at himself, tracing the tattoo with his fingers, smiling. Oh yeah, he knew how to get inside that bathroom. When he really wanted to get in, he'd whisper her first name: "Faye," he'd say, "let me in." He had the courage to put only the first three letters of her name across his chest, FAY, because it hurt too much to finish it.

"Let me in," he said.

"Hush now," said Mama.

It was hot underneath the covers. My body sweated; I had to pee. I waited for him to say her first name so I could go pee.

"Faye," he said, "let me in."

Slowly, the door opened. The light from their room hovered over my blanket. She held Daddy up and waited for him to prop himself against the dresser. He grunted, pointing one finger at her when she let him go; she had been holding him by the ribs. "I'm gone put my" he hiccupped, falling onto the bedroom floor, "my foot up your ass one of these days."

Mama closed the door. I could hear their activity, their words.

"Take your drunk ass to bed, niggah," she said.

Something fell on the floor. It did not make the sound of flesh. What noise I heard could have been anything at all: the open Bible at the foot of their bed, turned to the vocabulary of Deuteronomy, the mason jar that she housed the lizard in, a framed photo of Daddy in blue jeans, many things that carried the same weight but had their own privacy.

I heard Daddy crawling into bed, bitching about the acid in his stomach. He said he'd drunk too much soda pop at the Place, another name for the scrap yard: "Yeah," he said. What first turned out as laughter ended in a long cry. "What you got for me 'bout as sure as a white man paying me my money on time."

Mama mumbled something. The fallen thing was now in her hands. She was this type of woman. She picked up lost, broken things and tried to fix them. Her disappointment came when the thing could not be fixed.

"Get that light out o' my eyes," yelled Daddy.

In a short while, the locket carrying a small picture of my uncle Sugar, Daddy's only brother, was ticking against the bedpost where it had been since he'd been locked up in the Mississippi State

Penitentiary for raping a white woman. Mama's voice began to carry through the walls of the house. The sound of the locket grew louder. I visualized her reaching for it, trying to calm Daddy down, grab it from the bedpost so I wouldn't hear him fucking her.

It was said that Uncle Sugar had been dating Laurel Pillar for some time. Her granddaddy used to own Pillar's Grocery Store. But he died from a heart attack when he heard that a nigger had touched her.

And so the story went: Laurel asked my uncle to meet her behind the grocery one Friday. Like a fish to water, he went. Negroes had their vision. They said that a nigger didn't think when it came to a white woman. He got so caught up in that white skin that his dick got so hard that the flies wouldn't even touch him. That's what happened to my uncle. He got so excited about that white skin and white hair and white folks' blood that he took two other men with him to keep an eye on her granddaddy's place while he got him a piece of Laurel Pillar. Mr. Clyde, Laurel's daddy, had just come back from attending to his cows on Commitment Road when he caught them; the two who had supposedly been looking out ran off when they saw him coming.

The white folks had their version: Laurel Pillar started to scream. Justice Bates, one of the watchmen, and Uncle Sugar took turns raping her until there was blood from her pussy.

When word got out, Justice Bates was found on Commitment the next morning hanging from a branch in the widow's front yard. There was feces all over his body. They say the widow screamed so loudly that she lost herself. I knew very little about the other watchman, but Uncle Sugar was badly beaten. The white folks put the dogs on him. They found him hiding out behind the post office and beat him. He was almost blind by the time they finished with him. Daddy said that God gave his eyes back but he lost his manhood when they castrated him. Some say the white folks didn't kill him because cutting off a man's balls was far worse than kill-ing him.

It was hard for Daddy to look at Uncle Sugar after that. It had been years before he went to see him. And when the letters came from the penitentiary, he gave them to me to read; I stuffed the language of the letters inside my head. Uncle Sugar was a part of the system now. He was a number.

The ticking of the locket had stopped. Daddy was crawling off of Mama, his one arm reaching for the wall and resting it in the same fingerprints that she had left while waiting for him in the darkness. He let out a breath that settled in Mama's ears, some-how reminded her that she was a big woman and the need for him to hold her was out of the question now. The sheets told the story: the slow, gliding sound of them running up to the clot of blood in her breasts, over her protruding stomach. She was somewhere in that room pulling the sheets up on her with one tear falling from her eyes the way a woman is raped and left to her sorrow.

Daddy was sound asleep now. And Mama's hands were slid-ing beneath the covers to touch the rolls of fat there: she was counting them over and over again to see if one of them had gotten lost since she last touched them. I knew the pattern of her movements. I had seen her drag the bed across the room and push it against the wall where the moon didn't touch her body. And how she'd stand in the window for hours, naked, pacing the floor, looking down at herself to see how her stomach felt in the moonlight.

Her feet landed solidly on the floor. When the air returned to her lungs, she lifted herself from the bed and lit a match. The re-flection of the tiny light scurried beneath the door. The candle was lit now. She put it down on the dresser and brushed her crawling hair. The more she brushed, the heavier her cry. And before she knew it, she was at the edge of the bed again going through the pages of Deuteronomy. It was always Deuteronomy when she made love to Daddy for God. When she did it for herself, it was Ecclesiastes.

I held my pee.

chapter
three

It was Saturday morning. Aunt Pip's house was surrounded by magnolias. The petals were open, wide. The yellow parts had fallen onto the white, and they lay exposed like a woman's vagina at birth. Commitment Road was only a few miles from town, but there was a peace about it. It was safe to cry there. It was silently trapped by the earth.

Aunt Pip had been asleep all morning. The habit of her slow breaths touched the fabric of the pillows as her face turned sideways, her throat rising into a pattern of stillness, the white sheet pulled over her waist, her toes pointed, erect.

When she awoke, she found her way to the back room, where an old piano sat next to a square window. She stood with her back arched, her hands tapping lightly on the black and white keys.

"Put your hands on my shoulders while I play," she said. "Listen."

I felt her bones under my fingertips. She played wildly. I held on to her body as she shifted from me, the piano. It was so beautiful. The music filled the house. She moved into her notes with her hollow body pressing harder on the keys that were weak and required more agony from her fingers to move them along.

"Water," she said, "a tall glass."

I went to the cupboard and noticed a doe through the kitchen window. Her coat was the color of toffee after a child had played with it for hours. She moved toward the fig tree in the backyard and stroked her fur on the leaves. We looked at each other, the doe and I, staring each other in the eyes, as she turned away from me with her lungs pushing the breath from her belly.

"Maddy," said Aunt Pip, "the water."

Her arms hung from the side of the piano. I passed her a cold glass of water and she drank it; the lump in her throat rose as the water went down like a warm, sunlit river. The doe slowly made her way around to the piano room window. Her eyes were more piercing, lonely, full of something that was forced upon her—her vision.

"It's cold in this house," said Aunt Pip. "Light the stove."

Although it was springtime, her body was of a private temperature. I peeled a sheet of newspaper from the funnies. I had always been afraid to light a stove. Big Mama knew just how little to turn up the eye, just when to light the fumes.

"Be careful, now," said Aunt Pip. "That thing liable to set hell on fire if you touch it the wrong way. Be tender with it."

The stove was old. Three of the knobs were missing and turned by way of a hairpin stuck inside the veinlet. Only one worked properly. I found a box of matches next to the sink and held my breath before turning the knob. It clicked as I struck the match against the side of the box. The flame was blue at first, then it turned into a sweet-potato orange; I had done it.

"Turn it up, Maddy," she said.

"Yes, ma'am."

She pulled up a chair. It was clear that she had more strength. But she walked behind that chair with her backbone into it like she was a toddler taking a step for the first time. Arms outstretched, she reached for the sink, and the distance seemed farther than a game of tag when the winner felt it safe to turn around and look for the finger at his back, the urgent moment of time that became a cruel hoax to a runner who was a penny's waist from the finish line but never won the race.

"I'm tired, Maddy," she said. "I'm just tired."

She moved her reflection over the aluminum foil that Big Mama used to patch up a hole so the dishwater wouldn't leak out. She rested her elbows on the edge of the sink and looked deeper into her reflection. Her disfigured, drained flesh sank into the creases of the aluminum foil; she grew tired of looking at herself.

"Maddy," she said, "I think I want my chair now."

The morning hours were hardest. I separated the pills for her. Some were for pain. Others were supposed to treat the cancer. She hated taking pills. They reminded her of the titty machine. The doctors had given her articles, pamphlets, that included methods of dealing with the sickness with a healthy attitude, in exchange for death, suicide, depression.

"It's ten till nine," she said.

"Is the pain worse?"

"Pain is pain," she said, crouching over the blood in her breast.

The doe was beginning to make her way back to the kitchen window. The back door had a large rectangular windowpane. It was dirty. The images were blurry on the other side: the fig tree like a giant mushroom, the shape of Connecticut. Aunt Pip watched the doe through the mouth of her glass as the pills melted down upon her liver.

"She's been hanging around all morning," I said.

She ignored me. "Go up the road and tell Fat to send me a feel-good."

I stood there a moment.

"Do as you're told, child," said Aunt Pip.

I hadn't realized that I regarded Fat as simply the widow, a thing of consonants and vowels strung together through havoc, not as a woman who had right enough to be called by her first name, a woman who moved in her own company.

My legs shook beneath me as I stepped off the front porch. I looked up at the sky, back down at my shoes. There were trees, rows of honeysuckle on the sides of the road. I'd walked the same path with Big Mama, her telling me that when she was young she jumped on anyone's spine that had a curve it. "It was good luck," she said. "It was simply for good luck." And the master in the field, the rapist, who let his grandkids, children her junior, tell her what to do.

It had rained overnight. Occasionally, I turned around to view the shape of my footprints in the mud, the strange pattern of holes and earth water along the way.

The walk seemed long.

I plucked a small branch of honeysuckle from one of the bushes and peeled back the yellow part, with the elephant-shaped tusks at the end. The juice oozed out slowly as I glazed my tongue with it. It was sweet.

Fat's house was smaller than Aunt Pip's. There was an ax in the large oak tree where her old man Justice Bates had been hanged. The woodpile on the front porch looked old, stale, like it had been gathered winters before. It was stacked orderly like a man had come out of the woods and used his strength to save her the trouble, as if she had almost frozen last Christmas and wasn't going to let it ever happen again. The front yard was uncultivated, only spears of grass here and there. Nothing kept or proper about it. Just a piece of land that needed a woman's touch, her hand underneath its surface.

Out of three steps leading to the front porch, the middle one was loose. I jumped to the top one to get close enough to the door. My heart pounded. Finally, I knocked. Fat had a low, childlike voice. She had been reading aloud. I knocked again.

"Who is it?" she asked.

"Maddy."

"Who?"

"Maddy," I said. "Aunt Pip sent me."

She removed a tube sock from where the doorknob was supposed to be. She put one eye to the door before opening it. There was a long, flat braid going down the center of her scalp, the broken edges crawling behind her ears, close to her neckline. "Is she ailing or something?"

"She sent me for a feel-good," I said.

Fat was beautiful. Big Mama said that if a human being had a shadow to his eye, he was the devil. But Fat's eyes were solid; they were perfectly centered like the belly of a curved alphabet.

She turned to go into another part of the house, a bedroom perhaps. She shuffled through something. Nobody in Pyke County owned velvet except her. There was a velvet couch aligned with the rest of the objects inside the house: a green lamp next to one arm, a picture of Moses after coming down from the mountain, white-haired. A tiny house that smelled of scented talc and juniper that blended into something that arose when she was privately naked and squirting perfume on the back of her neck, just behind her ears.

She returned to the door with a brown bag in her hand: "Give her this for now," she said.

"Yes, ma'am."

She laughed with the wind in her mouth forming a small vol-cano down her throat. "I ain't that old," she said.

The door closed as I jumped off the front porch; the scented talc and juniper followed me along the way. The wooden sky—moving, suffocating now.

chapter
four

I was back home now.

"Wake up, child," Mama said as she pulled the curtains back from my bedroom window. "We need some eggs and cornmeal for supper. Your daddy's waiting."

It was a habit for her. Before breakfast was served, dinner was already on the stove. Between sitting Aunt Pip and taking care of things around our house, I was tired.

"Yes, ma'am."

"You get that girl up yet?" said Daddy from the kitchen table.

"She'll be out in a minute," Mama said. "She just a little sore from the lifting."

That was her way of saying it. I was just "a little sore from lifting" the sick. She had run from the responsibility of taking care of Aunt Pip herself. That's what happened. How much forgiveness did it take for a Christian to actually forgive? Mama was a Christian. Aunt Pip was a sinner. Christians were supposed to forgive sinners, but it didn't turn out that way. They were sisters. It wasn't as if God made special rules for such a relationship. Mama was the strong one. She took the shoes to the funeral home when Grandma died. Aunt Pip was the outsider, with only her fur and the guilt of sleeping with married men to keep her company. Neither Mama nor Aunt Pip had insurance. Just the sins of their flesh and the green earth beneath them.

"On credit or pride?" I asked Mama. The last time I went to the store with her, we didn't have enough money to buy a sack of potatoes. Mama stood at the counter and claimed that she had a five-dollar bill in her wallet before we left the house. She said that she had seen it with her own two eyes. Roberta Christian and her husband were next in line. They were the only black people in town with some money. Mr. Rye was Miss Roberta's father. Everyone called him by his first name. He lived across the road from us. His wife had been dead a long time. Neither one of them cared for sinners. After she passed away, I'd see him crossing the road at night to keep Miss Hattie Mae company. He was a deacon in the church, a respected man. His daughter, Roberta, kept her maiden name because she felt it blessed her. She and her husband were *blessed* enough to help Mama. Instead, they watched her go through her purse looking for a five-dollar bill that wasn't there to begin with. We were bound to see Miss Roberta again soon, coming over to the house with some gossip about the town folk's business. Time and time again, Mama let her in.

Mama paused for a moment. "Credit," she said.

Grandma called credit begging and pride what a person lost for begging. She had a reason for it. Laurel Pillar's daddy, Mr. Clyde, let us come back to the store not long before Grandma died. But Grandma refused to eat anything made, bought, or sold from the store. She said she had spent her life begging white folks for things that were hers to begin with. She ate from the garden behind our house and barely left her bedroom "to keep from ever having to call a white man mister ever again."

"But—" Before I could get anything else out, Mama's hand came flying across the wind. The side of my face stung.

"This is my house," she said. "Don't you back-talk me. If I didn't find a way to put food in this house, we'd all starve to death."

It was the second time she had ever hit me. The first was in church, when I laughed at the shit stain on Miss Hattie Mae's ivory slip.

"Yes, ma'am," I said, in tears now.

Her flesh shivered like Jell-O underneath her skirt, like she'd come so close to whipping me, but God stopped her. "I'm gone keep some kind o' order in this house," she said. "You best remember who came first in the world."

"Yes, ma'am."

At times, I felt so close to her. She was Mama. I talked to her. I loved her flesh like I loved mine. But we were losing each other somewhere. She needed me and I needed her. We just didn't know how to say it.

"You act like you don't know me, Maddy," she said with her hand over me.

"I know you, Mama," I said, louder this time.

She kept her hand over my face for a second, silently bitching beneath her breath.

"Now," she said, "get up and go to Pillar's with your daddy." She paused. "You act like I'm a spade sometimes. I ain't no spade."

She turned to walk out the door. "I might act like the devil ridin' my back sometimes," she said, "but I ain't no spade."

She didn't know her own strength. Once, when Daddy hit her, she didn't move one limb. She just looked at him and held the side of her face. He didn't know that the universe was inside her womb. The sun rose and set inside her belly.

"Yes, ma'am."

Those words saved my ass. If you didn't know what to say, as a Negro child, you always said "yes, ma'am." Those two words that took a small fraction of a minute to murmur saved me from a lot of shit that could have gone the other way around. When Grandma was alive, she'd be in one room and I'd be in another. But when she called me, I knew to say "yes, ma'am" all the way down the hall and around the corner, so she'd know that I respected her house.

I brought myself to my feet.

"Get a move on!" said Mama.

I pulled my nightgown over my head and placed it on the bed. My nipples were cold and hard like the tips of a Crayola before anyone had ever used it. "I'm coming," I said.

"What you doing in there?" yelled Daddy. "I ain't got all day."

Daddy was still banned from Pillar's Grocery. Mama and I were allowed to go because she had made a scene in front of the store one afternoon. A white man loved to see a Negro beg him for something, anything. Mr. Clyde stood behind the counter eating some buttermilk biscuits his wife had baked for him. Mama begged him, all right. She stood there in front of the "out to lunch" sign, crying for Mr. Clyde to let her in. Grandma was sick and she needed an elixir from the pharmacy located in the back of the store. After some time, he finally let us in. All that begging didn't do a damn bit of good. Because Grandma refused to take the medicine. The very thought of Mama embarrassing herself out there for a white man's remedy made her even sicker. No matter who it was for. Grandma died a week later.

"I'm coming!" I yelled.

Daddy was outside by now, revving up his truck engine. I pulled up my overalls and grabbed a shirt from a folded load of clothes. It was landscape green with a hand-painted daffodil on the shoulder.

"Mind Mr. Clyde," said Mama as I passed her; she was shelling a load of butter beans at the kitchen table.

I hated the sound of her voice. "Mind Mr. Clyde," as if I was to be a good nigger for him, a field hand or something without a language of my own. I didn't like her taking shit from the white folks, going to their house and cleaning their toilets with her bare hands. She did it for Daddy. If it meant keeping him, she did anything.

"Yes, ma'am," I said.

Daddy's full head of hair aggravated him at times. He would complain about the spiders from the scrap yard crawling around in his head. But he wouldn't dare cut it. His hair guarded him from the thought of having to look at the contours of his face, the low self-esteem of a man with no insurance.

I walked up to the truck. His head was turned. "Let me in," I said, tapping on the window.

"All right," he said, unlocking the passenger-side door and returning to fix his good arm for the drive. "Miss Hattie Mae sent some pecans over this morning. Be sure to thank her for 'em when we get back from Pillar's."

"I will."

Daddy drove toward Commitment, over five miles away.

"Why are we going this way?" I asked.

"Sugar sent me a letter," said Daddy. "I gave it to your mama. I figured you getting old enough to know what things mean."

"Maybe he wants to see you now," I said.

"It don't matter none," he said. "The government got him."

I wondered how many times he'd thought about the rape: Laurel Pillar's wild, tangled hair drawing a bridge across her shoulders, the castration.

"Daddy," I said, "you ever wonder where the dead go?"

"Naw," he said. "I don't have time to wurry 'bout where they go." He grew silent. "How Pip?" he said finally.

"The machines made her sick," I said.

He sneezed. The snot sprayed the palm of his hand as he adjusted the wheel with his knees. "Get that rag out o' the glove compartment," he said. "Wipe this shit off my face."

The handkerchief was covered with motor oil. The last time I'd held it in my hands, he was teaching me how to tell a monkey wrench from the pliers and other tools. He wanted me to know the difference in case his other arm went bad. I leaned over and wiped his nose.

"May be," he said, "but I ain't wurr'd. She got the head of a bull."

There was something between them. "I know."

He was a man who didn't own his own house. Everything we had once belonged to Grandma. It bothered him: a man sleeping in the same house with the spirit of a woman who mutilated a part of him. I saw it in his nerves, the way he wouldn't look me straight in the eye because nothing belonged to him. Everything from the bed he slept in to the plate he ate out of.

The sun shone through the windshield; the rays came down in spheres. We were approaching the house of Mr. Diamond, the postman. His lips were yet pursed. Big Mama's nipple had once been in his mouth. One winter day, his mother went to breast-feed him and discovered that her milk was frozen. She carried his pale body in her arms, crying. Big Mama stuck her hand beneath her own warm breast and opened his tiny mouth. She fed him so much that he became used to the brown breast, not the white one. Much later, after the milk of his mother's nipple had thawed out, he cried himself into a frenzy when she went to feed him. She put him back in Big Mama's arms, until the large Negro breast swallowed him. For this act of saving his life, he was grateful. But this was in no way to neglect the fact that the milk in her breasts was spawn from the penis of a white man. She was feeding Mr. Diamond the milk of a rapist. Everyone in town trusted him. Because he was the only white man who touched them. But I had my moments with him. There were times when I had stopped by the post office to check the mail, and he gave me a look that stirred the blood in my heart.

"She ever talk about me?" asked Daddy. He moistened the tip of a cigar with his mouth, his knees guiding the truck.

"No, sir," I said.

He eased off the gas. The engine hummed as he pulled into a wooded area close to where Mama and I had seen the cow in the road. "If she does," he said, "tell me."

The cows ran parallel to the fence. He put the truck in reverse and paused to light his cigar, striking a redheaded match on his jeans. I knew that he wanted to ask more questions, but it wasn't time. He was waiting to see if the machines were going to break up the solid mass of milk in her breasts.

"Is that a beagle?" he asked.

Whenever he saw a hunting dog in the road, he stopped to see if it had tags. If nobody owned it, he took it to the coon-on-the-log. During the springtime, he and some other men in town went out to a pond in Mount Herman, Louisiana, a small town on the Mississippi state line, to put their dogs up. It was a money game: ten to twelve wooden logs were rolled off the side of an embankment. Each man held the leash of his dog while folks bet money on the one they thought would be the first to kill the raccoon. On a good day, Daddy made good money. But Mama and I never saw it. He spent it right back up at the pool hall or trying to turn it over until it was gone. Sometimes he made up for it by selling the winning dog to another buyer. He never used the same dog twice. It was bad luck.

"Its leg is broken," I said.

He pulled over to the side of the road. "Get my rifle," he said.

He got out of the truck and walked over to the dog. It was white with a brown patch on its stomach. He turned it over to get a better look at the bad hind leg. The dog was female. Her nipples were thick; she was pregnant.

"Goddammit, Maddy," he yelled. "Did you hear me? Bring me the rifle!"

I took the gun down from the rack and passed it to him. "Here," I said, positioning the .22 on his shoulder blade. He knew how to use a rifle. He looked down the road both ways to see if any cars were coming, focusing on the nose of the gun.

"Get back in the truck, Maddy," he said. "Go on now. A mutt with a broke leg ain't good for nobody."

The earth called for the beagle. She knew that Daddy planned on killing her. She was quiet until her voice emerged into a fine, high shrill.

"Come on, now, gal," said Daddy, trying to coax her to her death. He walked over to the edge of the wood. "Be still."

The beagle turned over and used her three good legs to push off the fourth. She whined louder, gazing into the woods with her voice heavy in my ears.

The rifle rested on Daddy's shoulder. Then the beagle turned to me, as if there was something I could do to stop Daddy from killing her. Me? A child whose weekends were confined to watching over a sickness? Her tongue hung loosely from her dry mouth. Daddy aimed the .22 at her, his index finger on the trigger.

"Perfect," he said.

At that moment, Jesus Sanders was on his way up the road in a gold Cadillac that he called "sunshine." The seats were leopard-printed, and he always kept the outside greased. His hair was treated. One of the big girls at the pool hall permed it for him; I had gone to Factory with Mama once to pay off Daddy's gambling bill, and

Jesus was inside cursing out the woman, telling her how much of a bitch she was for burning up his scalp the way she did.

He took his time coming up the road. Jesus didn't get it in a hurry for nobody. He was a feared man. His Cadillac was his pride. Nobody fucked with his car. Nobody touched his gold. It wasn't his fault that men feared him. They were their own fools. All he had to do was drive around and smell sweet.

Daddy turned away from the dog. He opened the truck and put the rifle back behind the seat. "Jesus," said Daddy as Jesus blew his horn for the dog to move out of the way. She slowly crawled back into the woods. "Hey, baby."

"You just the niggah I wanna see," said Jesus. He loved to show off the gold tooth in the front of his mouth. He touched his clothes and raised his upper lip high on one side. His nose was flat and broad like the winding bone of a pork chop. Everyone feared him. Word had it that he'd killed a man in prison. They say that a number tried to cut his throat and missed his jugular by half an inch. The next morning the warden found the number hanging from his own belt.

"I got it covered, Jesus," said Daddy. "Ain't no need for bad blood now, baby."

Daddy kept his chest high around the house, but he was a pussy when it came to Jesus. He couldn't tell Jesus shit. He was a coward who needed a woman, a godly woman like Mama, so he could fuck her whenever he wanted.

"Motherfucker, if I don't see my money by nine o'clock tonight," Jesus said, "that's your ass."

He spoke through a narrow gap in the window, with his mouth up high to Daddy's ear. He had a good motor, a Cadillac motor.

"All right, baby," Daddy said to him. "Sure thing, baby. You know I'm good for it." He was fidgety. "Nine o'clock."

Jesus stared at me, as if he would have fucked me had I been just a little bit older. I slumped down in the front seat as he pulled off with a trail of dust behind him.

The nerves in Daddy's throat shook. He feared Jesus. Word had it that Jesus had been locked up in the penitentiary with my uncle Sugar for killing a man. Daddy wasn't a man killer. He took his anger out on what gave him power. But he respected men who killed other men. They frightened him.

"Jesus," he said, walking back toward the truck with his hand at his side. I carried his blood in my feet. It was the part of his life that he had given me: the outward pattern of the arch, the round heel that touched down prematurely.

He opened the driver's-side door. "Maddy," he said, "I'm taking you back to the house. Tell your mama that Pillar didn't have no eggs and the cornbread ran out some kind o' awful."

He drove like wildfire through the woods, praying about Jesus and his money. The cross on the rearview mirror was thick, clean. The last time I saw him use it was when his arm ached him. He woke up in cold sweats, saying that he felt his missing arm being lifted in midair. It bothered him for some time. The more he dreamed, the more he drank. The less he prayed.

"Sweet, Jesus," he said.

I cared more that I didn't have to go inside Pillar's and beg a white man for credit than I did about the debts he owed Jesus. It bothered me that Mama worked so hard for the white folks. Her bones so tired that she couldn't bend down to take the shoes off her feet. Blisters pussing up her toes so tough that when she grazed them with a safety pin, the infection ran clean down the side of her foot.

"I got you, baby," said Daddy.

A flock of birds sailed through the clouds, over us; the shadows of their wings over the hood of the truck. "Nine o'clock, Jesus," said Daddy, as he looked in the rearview mirror and talked to himself repeatedly.

The spiders were crawling into his scalp now, the poison rushing in. He needed some whiskey to keep him from thinking about the debt. Although Mama paid them, he wanted to do something on his own. His widow's peak invaded his forehead, as if the spider was beginning to make its web. "I gotcha, Jesus," said Daddy.

We passed Mr. Diamond's house. He stood with his hand pointing to one thing or another, his face the color of a dream.

Daddy spoke: "When you get inside, tell your mama that I had to do a man's business. You hear me?"

"Yes, sir."

"Be sure you do," he said. "Don't leave nothing out."

Mr. Clyde came toward us on a John Deere, pulling a load of cattle behind him. He sat high on his tractor as he came down off the hill. The wheels were huge, and the motor shook him; he occasionally turned back to check to see if the cattle gate was still attached. His jaws stuck out about an inch from his molars. Every time he turned around, he spat and wiped a code of tobacco on his sleeve. He grew closer, with the wind from the hill behind him.

"I'll be damned," said Daddy. "If it ain't Clyde Pillar yonder."

Mr. Clyde passed by, gazing into the truck at Daddy before spitting a hurl of tobacco on the windshield. It slid down the concave glass, coating a swirling heap of old fingerprints; they were mine. I read Mr. Clyde's lips: "Niggrah," he said. There were more words. Other words that were foreign in my house.

"Keep to the story," said Daddy, looking at Mr. Clyde in his side mirror. I turned to look at the load of cattle he was pulling behind him. Mammals put into the care of a man so angry. "If you feast your eyes on that hate one more time . . ." said Daddy.

I kept quiet.

The beagle was somewhere crawling back into the woods, the babies in her stomach churning underneath the weight of her fear.

"Hold on," said Daddy.

Daddy's woolly hair came down over the back of his ears. There was one time when he shaved it all off; he didn't want the spiders from the scrap yard crawling around in there and hatching eggs in his head.

"Jesus," he repeated, before pushing down harder on the gas pedal.

Mama was standing in Mr. Rye's front yard by the time we made it home. She went over there almost every day to see if he wanted something hot to go on his stomach. Even though he turned her down each time, she went anyway. She knew that he was old and set in his ways and that old folks didn't trust nobody's cooking unless they saw everything that went into the pot.

"Be sure and tell your mama what I said," Daddy yelled. "I gotta do a man's business."

I stepped away from the truck with the .22 in my hands. Mama was across the road standing in Mr. Rye's front yard, her hands propped up on her stomach. She knew that something was wrong, how Daddy moved when he owed a man his money.

"Chevrolet!" said Mama, yelling behind him. "Where you going?"

He was long gone. She took her hands off her stomach and started for the house. When her feet touched the road, she stood there a moment, the dust curling up through the trees. She paused before walking in the yard to grab the rifle out of my hands. She placed her cheek next to the barrel to see if it had been fired. "Don't just stand there, child," she said. "Where'd your sorry-ass pappy run off to this time?"

"He said to tell you that Mr. Clyde ran out of eggs n' cornmeal," I said.

She put one hand on her hip and sighed: "It's Jesus, ain't it?" she asked.

I didn't need to answer her.

"Lawd, have mercy," she said.

She looked down at the gun now, as if she had thought of something unkind. And shook her head; the words were getting stuck in there.

"Yeah," she said, "it's Jesus. I know it's Jesus."

She pointed the barrel of the rifle toward the ground and walked inside the house, shaking her head. Not more than a minute later, she came back out, tucking her wild hair underneath her Goodwill hat. She always wore hand-me-downs. All because Jesus came first in our house.

She opened her mouth and pushed a wind of breath from her lungs.

The rustling leaves of the pine trees above my head were falling in the wind, covering the ground sporadically. Mama was now praying over the steering wheel. Driving to Mr. Sandifer's, the pool hall, paying Daddy's debts with Jesus and others was making her shoulders decline, leaving her at an angle that forced a bad posture on her.

She rolled down the window. "Keep an eye on the butter beans for me," she said. "I got some business to tend to."

She cranked the car and revved up the engine with her heavy foot. After putting the car in gear, she flew off down the road. I walked toward the house, listening to the muffler hum past the river before making a last turn in the direction of the pool hall.

Even though Daddy never asked her for money, she knew that he'd never steal from her. She liked that in him—he never really asked her to pay Jesus. She did it because she loved him and wanted to have a man in the house, even if he did break all the rules.

chapter
five

It was the last day of school. Miss Diamond, the postmaster's wife, held the door open for the kids to catch their buses. I stayed behind for the third day of my detention. We had been studying Hitler. And when the test was given to me, I tore it apart. I didn't have to learn anything about Hitler; I knew about how he'd killed Jews, the babies and mamas and papas and grandmas and grandpas and sisters and brothers and uncles and aunts and cousins and future presidents and so on and so forth. His picture was the only one that I cut out of my encyclopedia. I burned it with one of my daddy's naked-lady lighters.

The other teachers were leaving. If our motto for the whole school year hadn't had anything to do with *Jesus*, Miss Diamond's clean, pale fingers would've come flying across my face. She was a small woman, her hair dyed the color of a natural disaster.

She had ordered me to sit in silence. I sat there watching the kids push Willie in his back. Nobody knew how old he was. We just knew that after the doctors took that glass out of his head, his grandfather went up to Jackson and got him, bringing him home in a blue blanket.

"Retard!" yelled the Mr. Goodbar bully, a kid whose heart I felt once to see if it was made out of a machine.

The other kids yelled at Willie from the yellow buses, throwing wads of notebook paper at him as he faded behind the crew of frantic bus drivers. There was blood on his spine; it had begun to form a dotted line up to his shoulder blade.

Miss Diamond sat at her desk and pushed her hair up from the back, looking out over the playground. "I watch you through the windows," she said.

"I know."

Her face was mechanical, the chin in the shape of an ice hook, the lips straight, almost inanimate. The lungs whispering quietly when the mouth was open. Not only her face but her bones. Her bones were mechanical.

Willie appeared from behind the buses, riding past the window again, and later returning to get a peek at Miss Diamond through the windows. She hated Willie. He worked for her husband every night at the post office for a bag of potato chips and a soda. She had been around him enough indeed. But she hated his condition. She looked at him this way, as if she wanted to crack his head open, where the scar was, and find his normality.

She ran up to the window screaming: "Get away from there!"

Willie saw her and smiled, looking down at his hands where the rocks had scraped them, causing them to swell. He jumped on his bicycle and moved back only a little. Miss Diamond turned away from him, her hand over her mouth.

I was tired of being silent: "I gotta go."

The worst she could do was tell Mr. Diamond to tell Mama the next time she stopped by the post office. I picked up my book sack and went for the door.

"Stop waiting for the world to apologize to you," she said, grabbing my arm.

I ran away from her. I kept running until I got to the end of the
hall, pushing the wide doors open and running past Willie and the
yellow buses, never looking back at the cinder-block building.

I relieved myself of my bag for a minute, sitting on the side of the
road as the yellow bus appeared in the distance behind me. It was
bus number forty-three. For some reason, Miss Birch, the driver,
drove the long way to get to everybody's house. If you lived by the
bridge, she passed the bridge at least three times before she dropped
you off. If you lived next to the post office, she passed it twice and
dropped you off on the way back. Like my father, she was an alcoholic.

I looked back to find Willie Patterson behind me, sitting on
his bicycle seat that was so high up that he had to lean down on
the handlebars to balance himself. The kids yelled, "Willie the
retard!" from the yellow bus, still throwing those wads of notebook
paper from the windows. He picked up speed for a moment, then
gradually put one foot in the bicycle spokes to slow himself down.

When he had been asleep in his mama's blouse, the nipple in
his mouth, he caught the wind of the world. The world killed him
when the glass went through his head. Both of his parents were
dead. The doctors in Jackson flushed the glass out with a hosepipe
and closed up his head. I wondered how they did that, if one of
the nurses held his head open and the doctor took out a sewing
needle and stitched up his brains. What happened to his thoughts
when his head was open? Where'd they go? The world had killed
his physical self. But his spirit survived when the angels came down
from the sky and wiped the dust off him; he was saved.

The yellow bus came to a complete stop in the road. Miss Birch
put one hand in the air and begged the kids to keep the noise down.
"You can ride the bus if you want," she said.

"I can stretch it," I said.

She saw Willie in her side mirrors. "Sure?"

The Mr. Goodbar bully balled his fists up at me. I would never see him again. His daddy had gotten a job making caskets down in New Orleans. His face was organized—like an atlas.

I looked back at Miss Birch: "I'm sure."

"Okay," she said, "I'll see you when school starts."

She drove away. The Mr. Goodbar bully ran to the back of the yellow bus and pressed his face against the window, pointing his fingers at Willie, laughing with his tongue pulling out from his tonsils.

"You coming?" I asked Willie. "Don't just stand there!"

He appeared shocked. "Diamond hurt Maddy?"

He repeated this sentence several times. I emptied my sack on the road, trying to find the piece of the aluminum foil that I had saturated with Vaseline for my cracked lips. "No," I said, blowing out a breath of fresh air, "Diamond didn't hurt Maddy. My lips dry," I said, finding the Vaseline and spreading it across my mouth.

Willie gradually put his feet on the pedals, those enormous Chuck Taylors weighing heavily on the tires. He made circles around me, stopping to put his index finger up to his mouth, imitating the way a lady puts her lipstick on. "Diamond hurt Maddy?" he asked again.

I hurriedly put my things back into my book sack, becoming aggravated. "No, Willie," I said. "Diamond didn't hurt Maddy."

"Diamond hurt Maddy," he said, shying away from me with his head to the ground.

He belonged to the stars now, so everything he said was serious, honest.

"What are you talking about, Willie?"

He pointed up toward the sky. "His eye cry too," he said, cradling his eyes from me as if I were going to hit him. "His eye cry like a itty-bitty baby."

"I won't hurt you," I said, walking up to him. He was so afraid that he fell off the bicycle. He no longer trusted. "The other kids hurt Willie 'cause Willie different. Not 'cause Willie bad."

"Not kid!" he said, looking as though he wanted to cry. "Man. Man hurt lady. Man hurt Willie!"

"I don't understand."

He jumped back on the bicycle. The long scar ran up the side of his head; he turned back around, screaming: "Man hurt lady!"

I wondered if Mr. Diamond or his wife had been beating him in private. Or his grandfather. But I knew that it couldn't have been the grandfather. He had already lost his only daughter. Willie was all that he had left. Something was missing. "Man hurt lady"; those words played time and time again inside my head, as Willie was in high speed now, his large Chuck Taylors pedaling through the dust.

Before I made it to the bridge by the house, I saw Jesus coming toward me, driving slowly. I wanted to show him the scratches on Mama's fingers from getting Mr. Clyde's clothes off the barbwire after a hard wind, how hard she worked to pay him. But I kept walking, growing nervous as I heard the sound of his tires screech on the warm ground beneath me.

He pulled up beside me.

"I don't bite," he said, rolling his window down.

"Just a piece to go."

The more I walked, the more he backed up the Cadillac, keeping his eyes on me and my fear, my anger. The tires rolled over the rocks and clumps of red dirt in the road. I walked faster, thinking about Willie Patterson and those words and wishing I had the speed of his bicycle. "Leave me alone!"

I looked Jesus straight in the eye. He stopped the car as I looked to see if Mama was standing out near Mr. Rye's house. She wasn't.

"Don't forget who I am," he said, laughing out loud in a deep, threatening voice. "I'm Jesus."

He spun off down the road with the powder of the earth be-hind him coating the air like a whore's perfume.

chapter
six

A tiny ray of light came through my bedroom window.

It was third Sunday at Owsley Sanctified Church. I stayed home to wait for Miss Hattie Mae's grandson, Landy Collins, to take down the hog pen in the backyard. Miss Hattie Mae was the mother of only one child, a daughter, who was pretty bent on not coming back to Pyke County. I think the place was too small for her. But she always sent Landy Collins to do carpentry work for the townsfolk: like the father of the Mr. Goodbar bully, Landy Collins was a casket maker down in New Orleans.

He was twenty-three years old with a muscular, well-to-do body. The bones under his charcoal skin fell into a perfectly chiseled form. Every summer, I'd sit by my window, waiting for the sound of his Ford to come flying up the road.

One time he stood outside my window and asked if he could touch me. I told him that his thing was too big. Truth was—I thought I'd end up in a pasture somewhere, butt naked like Big Mama, with blood coming from the hole between my legs, scarred.

Mama's body came into clear view. She struggled with a pair of stockings, trying to get them over her thighs in time for church. The more she bent over, the wider the hole in the panties. Her pubic hair darkened the coffee-colored stockings, until the vaginal pouch stuck out through the hole like the oval surface of a hard-boiled egg.

"I'll be tired when I get in from Owsley," she said. "See if Hattie Mae grandboy'll take you out to Pip's after supper."

She stuck the pubic hair back inside the stockings and pulled her skirt down, the lavender flowers heavily embroidered into the yellow. She then looked in the mirror and turned to one side, rubbing her hands on her blouse until they left the mark of a diamond on her clothes. "Look at me," she said, touching the fat of her stomach now. "I'll be waiting on hell to close up 'fore this go down."

She sat down on the bed, looking up at the ceiling. "The Lawd's been good to me, though. I can't complain."

Jesus passed by with the exhaust pipes hauling a line of smoke into the cold air. She pretended not to see him. I think it embarrassed her to chase Jesus around like she did. She went broke for Jesus. Jesus controlled her.

"He followed me," I said.

The glass vase was shattering now. She got up from the bed before the pieces hit the floor, her vagina leaving an odor in the air.

"I gotta go," she said. "You gone make me late for church."

The bottom was falling out of her shoes. She walked with her feet close to the ground; the others would notice, the women who worked just as hard as she did but had a decent pair of shoes to wear to church. If they had nothing else, they had a firm ivory slip, a couple of starched and ironed dresses, and a strong pair of hard-bottomed shoes that lasted a few years. They paid their debts to *Jesus* and nothing interfered with that. Mama went to church, but she gave her life to the wrong Jesus, the mortal one.

Shortly after she pulled out of the yard, Daddy appeared at my door. He had begun to smell like milk. He had been doing extra work for Mr. Diamond, who had bought fourteen cows from Mr. Clyde. "Where your mama?" he asked.

"Church," I said.

He thrust his hips forward and rested his backbone on his buttocks, as if the work had been beaten into him subconsciously. "What time she coming home?" he asked.

"Didn't say."

He went to their bedroom, closing the door like he had been waiting for her to leave all along. He was counting money. I knew that sound like I knew my bones. He was sighing now, stuffing the money into his pockets.

Not long ago, some men came down from Chicago. He had already owed Jesus money. He didn't care too much about his life. Time and time again, he went back down to the pool hall. Each time they put him out, telling him that he couldn't come till he paid Jesus. But they'd let him in sometimes, when Jesus was out of town and the cool cats were in there. The ones who didn't talk, because they knew that he would play himself, that if Jesus caught him in there, he would kill Daddy. Sure. Jesus could have easily come to the house and gunned him down in the front yard. But I think it meant something to him, under all that tough skin of his, that Mama worked so hard to pay him. I believe that if he hated Daddy for anything, it was because he let his woman scrub toilets to pay his debts. She was the only one who could make Jesus wait for his money. He trusted her.

Daddy opened the door. "If she get here 'fore I do," he said, "tell her I went to see a man about a mule."

He was lying again. It was the way he turned his eyes away from me when he said this, his unpicked Afro, the alcoholic sweat on the corner of his upper lip.

"Yes, sir."

He walked back up the hall, breathing hard, loose. He hadn't yet opened the kitchen door. The wind outside whistled into a strong force against the shutters. He stopped somewhere over the kitchen window, as he often did, thinking of the day he fucked Aunt Pip, the fire-engine-red lipstick falling from her hand, settling on the ground like a bottle of aspirin.

He returned. "Just tell her I went to see a man," he said.

He coughed long and hard. The sound of it echoed throughout the walls of the house. He then went outside and cranked the truck before stepping out of it to check the wires. He was in a world of his own. Head bent low, he looked the engine over and tapped an exposed cylinder. "It's been a long time," he yelled, raising his hand to Landy Collins, who had walked over to greet him.

Landy had grown thicker. His shoulders high in the air with the confidence of a white man. His large hands, swollen from work. His face—a perfect mask that fit over the bones with a lasting impression. Beautiful.

Daddy had begun to talk about his days of infidelity, the flesh of a whore's vagina, the rawness of it. He leaned away from Landy Collins and made a circle with his hand.

"Landy," I whispered, stepping back from the window and looking at myself in the mirror. Maybe one day, I thought, I would let him pet my fur. It hadn't yet grown into a full shade of wires like Mama's. I could have never shown it to him the way it was. It would have embarrassed us both.

He and Daddy were under the hood of the truck, both tapping something electrical. "That should do it," said Landy.

At the sound of his voice, I touched myself inside. The way I thought he would have touched me had I given him a chance. His voice grew deeper, louder.

"Maddy," yelled Daddy from the cylinders, "Landy's here."

I came and my legs gave out, as I shook recklessly in my clothes, my fingers slippery. In my desire, I heard Landy Collins say the word: "Pussy," he said.

"Be out in a minute," I said, resting my body on the mattress in an effort to regain my strength.

Later that day, Landy Collins made it to the backyard. He stood next to the hog pen, measuring everything with care. The orange sun in his eyes, picking up the hammer when necessary. His muscles were circular. He turned his face upward, exposing the jawbone.

My flesh was soaked with sweat as the pot on the stove boiled over, steaming up the house in a thick fog. I went to the refrigerator and stood there for a while, watching a cube of ice melt on my skin. I took out a lemon and cutting board, sitting them down on the kitchen table. The table wobbled badly. Daddy had been drunk when he built it; it was the only thing he could afford to give Mama as a wedding gift.

I cut myself.

The blood came down in ripples over the blade.

"Maddy," said Landy as he made his way through the back door.

He walked toward me, the heat from his body rising into a translucent cloud in the air. He was dark like a nightmare in the middle of the night that no one could pull herself out of.

The blood from the blade had dripped on the floor, the trail making a dotted pattern, the corpse of a dragon. Or a dinosaur.

"What happened to you?" he asked.

"Nothing," I said, hiding my finger behind my back, the blood cold.

"Let me see."

He cornered me against the wall, the sweat from his balls rising in the fog. And suddenly, as if without thinking, he took my finger in his mouth and sucked the blood from it.

The kitchen was silent now.

He walked back out to where the hog pen was coming down, my blood in his mouth.

It was dark outside now, active. The dirt was dry, and the government men had bush-hogged the weeds onto the side of the road. The earth wasn't orange anymore. The insects were out parading on it. Their voices spoke to one another with a language heard, absent a vowel, a consonant, a constant dialect. Yet I heard them fucking around in the darkness.

Landy Collins pulled up to take me to Aunt Pip's. He lit a cigarette and checked to see if the headlights were on. His broad shoulders were elevated high above the steering wheel. The side of his face was fragile, like a picture of Egypt.

The truck picked up speed. And when we got to the stop sign at the end of the road, I thought of the pregnant beagle. She was somewhere lying on her belly in the darkness, coping with the atmosphere as it was. The earth was growing moist underneath her. She had given birth and kept the babies quiet with her milk. Saved by Jesus.

"Mama says that if you cut down all the trees in Mississippi, you'll find Negroes from here to kingdom come," I said.

"Not just Mississippi," said Landy Collins, looking through the headlights. "Anywhere you find a tree, there's a Negro hanging from it. You might not see him, but he's there."

The roaring of cattle was in the air. They came running toward the barbwire fence, back again. Their bodies as loose as a maid in a white man's kitchen.

"You want me to touch you?" asked Landy.

"No."

"Yeah, you do," he said. "You like it when I touch you."

"No, I don't."

He laughed. "Take off your shoes and put your feet in my lap."

I was unsure at first. But there was something about him. I knew not what. This was the part that I had gotten from Mama, the weakness of being ordered.

"Trust me," he said.

By this time he was circling the arch in my foot.

"I'm too young to trust."

"No," he said, "you just green. Anything green is faithful. It's been that way since the beginning."

His silhouette curved into a gradual slope. I had seen him in a global atlas when I found Uganda with my own finger.

We were nearing Commitment Road.

"Ain't that Fat's place?" asked Landy.

"Yeah," I said, putting my feet back inside my shoes, "how you know Fat?"

"I used to come out here and stack her up for winter."

"What happened?" I asked.

"She stopped seeing me as help and started seeing me as a man," he said.

"That ain't reason enough."

"It is when a woman that big takes baths outside her house butt-ass nekked," he said. "That's just too much woman for me."

Aunt Pip had left the porch light on. The curtains were pulled back, as if she had been waiting for me, lifting herself to the window, listening to the sound of the tires on the road to see if Mama's car was turning in.

Landy pulled up in the yard. "Get inside," he said.

I stepped down from the truck, leaving him. I felt him watching me as I turned to find him standing beside the Ford, his hand resting on the hood.

chapter seven

The earth was warm. Mama and I were on our way to Aunt Pip's when we saw a group of cattle grazing in the open field ahead of us. A white man walked among the cattle with a bucket in his hands. He looked up at the horizon and wiped his brow, sitting the bucket under one of the cow's stomachs and pulling her nipples. The cow began to kick. He stood up beside her and tried to calm her down.

Mama saw this and touched her breast with her free hand. "That cow got the sickness," she said. "You can look at 'er and tell it. Her milk done went bad, and now her titties sick."

The white man put the bucket under the cow's stomach and squeezed her nipples again. The cow moved its head wildly and broke out into a run that sent it to the far end of the field.

"Tol' you," said Mama.

We were approaching a stop sign. Across from us was the couple, the husband and wife who had followed Mama and me on Commitment Road. The wife was a stiff woman. Her face was an abstract painting, the mouth barely moving, the teeth upset by a protruding bridge. She looked at her husband, the driver, as if her neck was strictly mechanical. Words came from her tight lips, but he did not respond. He was just as rigid, as if since that day, something horrible had happened between the two of them that drew their feelings apart.

"I got life in me," said Mama. "Thank you, Lawd. I got life in me."

These are the last words I heard from her before getting out of the car and watching her box-shaped head turn away from Commitment, in the direction of home again.

Aunt Pip was in the kitchen, facing the rectangular window, looking out into the backyard. The weight was slowly returning to her bones. And the mirrors that I had taken down were up again.

"What do you see?" I asked.

"All the things I missed while I was asleep," she said.

The fragile nightgown clung to her. It was white with green stitches along the hem. Her hands were in her lap, the cloth dipping from the burden of them.

A fly buzzed around us. It landed near the edge of the windowsill. For a moment, it sat there with its wings fluttering, its hind legs like a protractor. The purple eyes, the large pupils.

"If your titty ever get sick," said Aunt Pip, "don't take it to men."

Her pattern of breathing forced the fly into the air again. Its wings settled on the kitchen counter, disturbed.

"God made doctors," I said.

She laughed. "I know. Doctors and men who'll never know what a machine can do to a woman."

I recalled the first night with her—how she talked about her titty going into a compressor, the doctor sitting on a stool and looking at her lump through a microscope. The big words he used. Words like "malignant" and "benign" and what I'd discovered in the dictionary: "carcinoma."

The sincerity of the subject returned to her face, as it had before when her breath annoyed the fly. "A lady I knew," she said tenderly, "I'd see her at the grocery a time or two, and folks used to wonder why she fed her baby out in the open." Her hand was over the hanging breast, the one shaped like the head of a swan. "She tol' 'em babies wadn't meant to go hungry. And if she could help it, she'd feed hers till the milk run sour."

She lifted her leg and pressed her toes on the horizontal edge of the window. The color of her skin returning.

I thought about my father. He wasn't drunk when he told me about the cattle, the sour lump coming out of the nipple. A hard lump the color of a white Crayola, the one that I never used because it was already dead.

"That's just what happened to her," said Aunt Pip. "Her milk went sour, and the next thing we knew she was laying up in the cemetery with her titty missing."

The disease had fallen into the milk bucket now. In my head, Daddy was picking it up in his hand, measuring it against the earth.

The air between Aunt Pip's legs was rising. It wasn't of juniper or petals from the magnolia tree, but of Mama's fur; a trail of her life passing through her abdomen, a sweaty odor of a woman with a past for reaching for fallen things.

"The sun's coming up," I said.

"I know," said Aunt Pip, getting up from the chair.

With her face to the rectangular glass window, she took one hand and touched the flesh underneath her arm. She never talked about the lump there or the brick-colored mass that oozed out of her nipple on occasion. She pulled the gown over her head and stood with her body pressed against the translucent glass, dropping it at her feet.

"You ever wonder where God is up yonder?" she asked.

"No," I said, "but I taste Him every time I eat a piece of butterscotch candy."

She laughed and turned her face to one side, her cheek in the center of the rectangle, and began to pound her jawbone on the hard surface. She did not do this violently. I believe she wanted to hear the life of a solid bone, something besides the sound of a compressor coming down on her breast to categorize it.

"It's still inside o' me," she said. The thumping stopped. "They say you don't know when your life is leaving you. You can't feel the disease spreading to other places." She brought her hand down from the swollen hill underneath her arm. "But that's a lie. I was born perfect. Every part of me in place. I know when something ain't right. It wakes me up in the middle of the night the minute I forget it."

I believed her. Daddy once said that a leaf had come loose from a tree in front of him. And he could feel the spirit of his missing arm rising in the wind to protect him.

Aunt Pip's hair was not growing back the way that it had left her. It was thin, dry. She stood with her back arched; her shoulder blades in the shape of a butterfly.

The next morning, Fat had come through the door with a glass of whiskey in her hands. She took a seat next to Aunt Pip's bedside. I watched, listened.

"When I tell you that nigger was wired, he was wired," said Fat. "He used to say he had balls big enough to throw over his shoulder."

Aunt Pip's eyes widened when she heard Fat speak, her head uncovered. "Yeah," said Aunt Pip, "I knew that fool was lying when he said he had kin on Prytania Street. We had New Orleans shut down then. And we ain't never seen the likes of him hangin' around the place."

Fat smiled. "Sho," she said. "That nigger couldn't say he didn't love me. He thought I was crazy as a Betsy bug, but he loved me.

That's for damn sure." She lifted her skirt to the pubic hairs in her panties. "What's not to love?"

They both laughed out loud. Aunt Pip loved Fat. They shared something on Commitment that nobody in Pyke County would ever understand. She and Fat laughed through the hatred the county felt for them, laughing about the men I never knew existed.

Aunt Pip gradually pushed herself to the wall behind her. "Remember that chocolate motherfucker who kept telling the boys at the pool hall that he wanted my hand?"

"Yeah," said Fat, "I remember him. That bastard didn't have a pot to piss in or a window to throw it out of." She laughed again, holding herself by the stomach. "What was his name? Slim?"

"That's it!" said Aunt Pip, snapping her fingers. "I told that nigger that if he didn't tie his shoes, I'd kill his ass quick as the day is long." She tapped Fat on the arm, pointing through the window past the tiny lizard that lay there. "You should've seen that fool running out through the field yonder."

"Lawd," said Fat, "if I'd seen it with my own two eyes, I believe it woulda been over for Fat. I mean over."

They laughed out loud. The house was growing warm. Springtime was coming and the magnolias were restless. I was thinking about the letter from Uncle Sugar that Mr. Diamond had long since delivered, the one Daddy spoke about the morning we saw Jesus. And why Mama hadn't yet opened it; it lay at the foot of her bed, next to the pages of Deuteronomy.

"Ooh," said Aunt Pip, snapping her fingers, "I wanna go to New Orleans. Hell, I oughta just take my black ass to the pool hall 'n' give them niggers a piece o' my mind!"

She then looked down at a small oval mirror next to her bed and pushed herself back against the pillows again, her face pained.

Fat noticed her embarrassment: "Pip," she said, "you don't wanna go down there nohow. That place all ate up with crabs!"

Aunt Pip closed her eyes. "Well," she said, "that's bad for somebody, ain't it?"

Fat grew silent then. "You been wearing that lipstick I give you?"

"Every now and then," said Aunt Pip.

"Damn, Pip," said Fat. "Why you think I give it to you? All you wanna do is lay up in this house and give up on yourself."

"I can't help it sometimes."

"You can't help it?" said Fat, laughing. "The Pip I know ain't got shit to do with help. She stubborn as a mule."

"I'm coming out o' it."

"You better," said Fat. "I'm going crazy in that house all by myself."

This is why Pyke County had branded her. They'd heard it through the grapevine that she wrote letters to a dead man. Her dead husband, Justice Bates.

"All right, Fat," said Aunt Pip, pulling the curtains back. "I'll try."

"Give me that sunshine I'm used to," yelled Fat. "Go 'head!"

Aunt Pip rehearsed the lines. "Give me a pig foot and a bottle of beer."

Fat laughed so hard her laughter got caught in her throat and she coughed. "That's what I'm talking 'bout. Billie's blues."

"Don't get me started, girl."

"Before the day is over," said Fat, "I'm gone have to call the law!"

She stood up and lifted her skirt again and kneeled to the floor, her ass in the air. Her face was magnetic, heroic.

She and Aunt Pip smoked wrinkled cigarettes the rest of the evening, talking about New Orleans and how they were going back someday, while they were alive.

chapter
eight

The following morning, I was on Aunt Pip's front porch watching her through the window, the curtains flying into a cloak over her. She looked like the pictures inside the encyclopedia, the small drawing of a fetus before it had fully developed, the thumb inside its mouth.

Mr. Clyde was in the vast field next to the house, talking to Mr. Diamond. They stood in the green, shaking and nodding their heads, pointing to the cows on the opposite side of the road. I could vaguely hear them over the distance. They stood like white men. Their faces diagonal to each other, turning sideways when the subject matter was important. And leaning back against their vertebrae, putting pressure on their vertebrae with an air about them.

All the white men in town knew one another. Mr. Clyde, Mr. Diamond, Daddy's boss, Mr. Sandifer, other white men. We'd be going up to the grocery store and they'd all be outside talking about the differences between Chevys and Fords. I wished my daddy could just sit around in his pride, debt-free, and shoot the breeze about something so trivial as miles to the gallon. White men had it easy. They worked just enough to call themselves men and went home and laid across their flatironed sheets with their long legs propped up on the bed rail, chatting and kissing the cleanliness from their white wives. A black man didn't have time to be gentle with his woman. He had enough stress already. Staying alive was stressful. Going to work and having to call a white man "mister" was stressful. Waking up with that black skin and that nappy black head that showed to the roots, those rough black hands that they couldn't do nothing about, was enough stress to break him, no matter how much man he thought he was.

Daddy pulled up in his truck, walking up through the machines. He saw me there on the front porch, his face blank. The white men had seen me too, pointing their fingers at the ground and looking up into the clouds for rain.

It seemed to me that my daddy had no more pride in himself than to let Mr. Clyde drag him around the county when he wanted to: stop by this white woman's house, cultivate her garden, work your fingers till the blood comes running down because you're the nigger whose brother took my Laurel. This is the way that it was. A diseased human being resorted to anything, I thought, even if it meant bowing down to the feet of his worst enemy. If it could get them what they wanted, no matter what that something was; it was worth a try.

Mr. Clyde's lips moved. He pointed to a clear spot in the field. Mr. Diamond, who looked at me from afar with squinted, threatening eyes, scratched his scalp and seemed to be compromising with Mr. Clyde. He pointed toward another vacant spot in the field, and they both nodded.

"Right here," Mr. Clyde said loudly, bending down to pull up a fistful of brown dirt in his hands. "This is a good place for it."

Mr. Diamond cranked the John Deere. He stretched his legs out over the pedals and shifted the gears before looking out below him, into the sky. The seat was high. I don't think he was really used to the work. Mr. Clyde gave him a few pointers, and he gripped the wheel, maneuvering the heavy machinery into a well-thought-out routine: a little to the edge of the wheel, a quick right, back down through the dirt, gutting the center. Occasionally, he looked back to make sure the land was coming up behind him.

"Come on here now," he said to Daddy, raising his voice high over the motor.

Daddy seemed so small, as if he couldn't have kept a fly from hurting me. He walked behind Mr. Diamond, pulling a wheelbarrow with his arm, stopping every other step to fill up the holes with cow manure.

"I gotcha," he yelled, pausing to pull a leather glove from his back pocket and laying it flat on the ground. He turned it over several times, positioning his hand with it before sliding his fingers through.

Mr. Clyde stuck his hand into the fertilizer and laughed out loud, talking about how he had found himself a good one. His letters curved in the wind, the sound of his voice widening deeper into the air, as the length of the field stretched it over the green. He marched up to Daddy with his arms swaying, stopping abruptly.

He said something to him. And all I could make of it was: "Do you hear me?" Daddy looked him in the eyes when he spoke to him, his chest high to him. Mr. Clyde kept his finger pointed in his face for a second, down to the ground, back in his face.

Right now, Daddy was thinking of the letter at the end of his bed, the numbers in the penitentiary that Uncle Sugar was fighting off. Because they knew that he was a man with no balls. Because they knew of the only penetration he had left in his body, the part leading up to the intestines, the fall of a man.

"Maddy," said Aunt Pip, yawning from the window, "who's out there?"

"Men," I said. "Go back to sleep."

She had heard Daddy's voice out there. There was something about the experiments of the machines that caused her to rely on instincts, to recognize the sound of a white man coming down on the handicapped. The same way Grandma had known that my father had been cheating and fed his arm to an animal. The same animal that he had beaten, battered.

Daddy looked down at the pasture, sprinkling the fertilizer and looking back up on the front porch. I smiled at him. That day when he asked me about Aunt Pip, I saw something in his eyes. He held something for her deep inside him. A memory that a married man couldn't dare share with his wife. One of those loose memories that a man couldn't control by himself. He needed the object of his memory to clear him of its thought. If only he could see it, if he could just lay his eyes on the thing that captured him, everything would make sense: the alcoholism, the long nights at the pool hall, wanting to make love to Mama only when he was drunk and didn't care what she looked like. He walked closer to the fence but stopped, the harder the white men came down on him.

Time went by. The clouds gathered above us. It began to sprinkle, and the water flowed on the rocks with a collective noise that sounded throughout the woods, seasoning the pine trees with an emerging faint mist.

"Get the clothes off the line," yelled Aunt Pip, now looking through a shoe box of things. "I smell it coming."

I ran around the back of the house barefoot. The moisture slowly seeped into the earth, the rain soaking my hair at the roots.

It began to pour. The rain pounded upon the tin roof, running alongside the edge of the house in thick streams. Daddy and the white men talked loudly over the John Deere. I gathered the clothes in my arms and ran back inside the house.

As I was closing the windows, I saw Mr. Diamond shift the John Deere; Mr. Clyde was behind him, driving his pickup. Daddy signaled for him to roll his windows down, the fertilizer in his hand drowning. The next thing you know, he was running toward the house. I quickly closed the curtains. The John Deere hummed loudly, a short pause between gears, a higher shift, the sound of Mr. Diamond leaving the field.

"Listen to that," said Aunt Pip, closing her eyes to draw a breath. "God is crying."

There was a knock at the door. It was Daddy. He shifted his feet on the ground the same way he did when he owed Jesus his money. He whispered her name in a loud, flat whisper. "Pip," he said.

Aunt Pip touched the living breast, the head of the swan pointing eastward. "Don't answer it," she whispered. "Please."

Daddy knocked harder. Although her hair was beginning to grow again, she reached for the pink scarf on the Styrofoam bust, covering it. She had not seen him since Grandma's funeral, when her hair was down her back, full. Now the cancer had not yet claimed her life, but the experiments had taken her energy, the old energy that he remembered.

"Maddy," said Daddy, "it's your daddy. Open up."

"Don't," whispered Aunt Pip.

Daddy shifted his feet again, the shadow of them forming a triangle. "I know you're in there," he said.

Aunt Pip covered her face. She would have died rather than let him see her that way. Her eyes sunken into a hollow, oval-shaped bone.

It was quiet.

Then the horizontal boards on the front porch began to moan. Daddy was close to the curtain, his face almost metallic, as if the arrangement of the things in the house would subconsciously speak to him. He stood there waiting for something to announce itself, to please him. He knocked awhile longer before stepping off the front porch and back into the rain.

"Thank you, Lawd," said Aunt Pip.

She opened the curtain a little and saw him running back to his truck, shielding the downpour with his arm.

Aunt Pip eventually went to sleep again. I stayed up with her that night, catching her leg each time it rolled off the side of the bed, putting it back under the covers, so the blood wouldn't go bad in it.

chapter
nine

Summer was ripe now. The earth was beginning to heat up the Mississippi dust. Time was passing almost rapidly, it seemed. And I was at the end of Commitment Road talking to God when I saw Mama's car coming toward me, passing the cemetery. When she pulled up, her skin was the color of butterscotch and her mouth was calm, as if *Jesus* had come down off the wall and answered her something.

"Get in," she said.

"Where we going?" I asked.

She looked at the triangular roof of Aunt Pip's house, the open window. "Sugar's," she said, as if he was a free man.

I remembered very little about Uncle Sugar except for what Mama had told me. He liked fast cars and women. Smoked a lot of the feel-goods. Hung out in the cities that other Negroes had to bribe their way into. He was a learned city slicker. He knew a lot about Jesus and hung out on Factory Road just as much as Daddy did. The difference is that he owned Factory. He didn't take no shit off the Negroes. And he didn't cry none over money. Everybody's money was his money. The folks at the pool hall thought he was a superstar. He shared what he had. Bought drinks for the boys and let them get over fifty dollars in the hole before he said anything about it. No, he wasn't a bully like Jesus. He respected everybody and wanted them to respect him the same. Daddy called him "Sugar." When he did talk about him, it was always "Sugar this" and "Sugar that" and "Some boys from New Orleans came to the pool hall asking about Sugar and I had to tell 'em what happened to him. It killed me to have to tell 'em that the white folks took him downtown."

We stopped by the house to pick up Daddy. I didn't want to go. My uncle was a rapist. That's the whole of it. Some white woman got her "hole stretched out by a horse-dicked Negro, and the white folks gave him a number." It didn't matter who said it. It didn't matter how long he was locked up. Once a Negro went down for raping a white woman, it could have been the era of a new millennium, a new century, a decade, he'd always be branded for taking the cleanliness from her. No, I didn't learn that from those white scientists. I didn't have to. All you had to be was born black to know that.

Mama said that I needed to go. That Uncle Sugar wanted to see how life had been treating me. I took it that she had opened the letter at the foot of the bed. I suppose she felt guilty for having it sit there in her bedroom and collect dust when a man's life had been detailed in the words. A man who hadn't seen the sun in years, who was privately suffering like she was and had only a Bible, a free Word, to help him keep his sanity.

"Maddy," Mama said, looking at me in the rearview mirror, "did you remember to pack those sandwiches?"

"Yes, ma'am."

"Stop by the post office, Faye." Daddy unfolded his wallet and took out a toothpick. He pricked a piece of hair from the tip of it and put it in his mouth. "Diamond say he got some spare change for me, since I helped him tend the cows."

"Chevrolet," said Mama, letting off the gas and taking one hand from the wheel, putting it on her hip, "you do what you *have* to do for the whites. They don't do a damn thing for us. Besides, that Pillar girl got this town hog-tied."

He had threatened her one night. He told her never to say "Laurel" around him. So she said "that Pillar girl" instead, as if Laurel had done her something, as if she was nobody's child and deserved what she had gotten.

"Shit, Faye," he said, "can't I have something for myself? Every time I get up, you steady trying to knock me down. Goddamn."

"You just a nigger to him," she said, in one of those rare responses when the housework had gotten to her.

"All right, now," he said.

"That mean you trust him," said Mama, nodding and reassuring herself that she was the right one.

"That don't mean I trust him. That mean if anybody, I mean anybody, don't care what color, tell me that they got some money for me, I'm going to get it."

"That mean you trust him," she said, leaning her chin forward.

"How you know, Faye?"

"'Cause we wouldn't be going if you didn't trust him," she said.

"You say that," he said, "but if I got some money in there, you gone be the first one to have your hand out asking for some o' it."

"Is it green?"

"What you mean is it green? Yeah it's green."

"Then I can work with it," she said. "You don't seem to have no problem putting a hand on mine."

"Watch yourself," he said. "You hear?"

The tires screeched as she pulled over onto the grass. "I know you think my head ain't got no bottom in it," she said, turning to look him in the face. "Yeah," she said, pointing at me, keeping her eyes on Daddy. "I clean them white folks' toilets. I scrub their floors. But I don't do it for you. I do it for my child. Maddy is *my* child. You may have helped her come into this world, but dammit, she's mine. All mine. And as long as I see a book in her hand and she's standing up to that Miss Diamond up there in that school yard, I'm gone keep on scrubbing them floors and saying 'yes, ma'am' and 'no, ma'am' and cleaning them floors so tough that I can see my child's glory in 'em. No, Chevrolet. It ain't my glory. It's my child's glory when my face shine."

She cried in her hands. She had never mentioned one word about my back-talking Miss Diamond on the last day of school. Or the many times I'd been in detention for having my own beliefs. She never talked about it. Just a mother, a strong woman who carried her pride in her hands, working hard so I wouldn't have to ever go through life without my own self-learned education. I loved her.

She pulled back onto the road, turning the radio up as loud as it would go. "Yeah, Chevrolet," she said firmly. "I hear."

"Slow down, Faye," said Daddy, "you gone pass the post office up."

Daddy used that harsh voice of his to remind her that he was still a man. He straightened up his shoulders and looked at her like he meant his words. She hadn't taken anything from his manhood by talking like that in front of me. A black man had to be a man at all times. He didn't own anything else. Nothing else belonged to him.

"All right, all right," she said, slowing down.

She pulled up to the post office. The door had two small bells hanging from it to let Mr. Diamond know that someone was coming in. He had a habit of sleeping. It seemed like every time anybody went in there, he was sitting down in his recliner snoring out loud. He'd jump up when the bells rang, wiping the matter from his eyes.

"Go inside," said Daddy.

"Yes, sir."

It embarrassed Daddy to have to ask Mr. Diamond for the money. Daddy was a gambler. What sense did it make to pay a gambler? Gamblers didn't last long. They hustled their green and spent their green as fast as they made it. Green didn't sit in their hands. They spent it and prayed for the gold. *Jesus* didn't bless gold. And Daddy knew that Mr. Diamond wasn't about to give him the money. Please. The brother of a convicted rapist? Never.

The bell rang when I opened the door. Mr. Diamond rose up from the fragile recliner, awakening himself from a deep sleep. Once he saw it was me, his facial expression showed disgust. He walked away from the counter, grabbing a small towel from a drawer on the other side of the room. His receding hairline made an arch around the crown of his skull. The upper part of his torso was large, like he used to be a bodybuilder but stopped working out and the calories caught up with him. His stomach hung over his belt, and when he bent down, the long, winding hairs on his back turned blond in the fluorescent light. I imagined him naked sometimes, with his testicles lifting his penis to the forefront. I paid more attention to him now, since my mama's words and the magnitude of them. All those details that meant nothing to me before meant something because now they had to. I had to know what type of white world I belonged to, paying closer attention to mannerisms.

The floors were white as a ghost. Willie had them shining so Mr. Diamond could walk across them with that post-office ink on the bottom of his shoes, dragging along the linoleum.

"Can I help you?" he asked sarcastically, walking back toward the counter.

"Forty-three, please."

He knew the routine. I said the box number. He gave me the mail. It seemed he wanted more time to look at me with those hateful eyes, to remind me of that dreadful day I had with his wife, Miss Diamond.

"Let's see," he said, going over the numbers with his glasses hanging from the tip of his nose, "forty-three. Forty-three."

He walked carefully through the place, leaving the numbers and going to take care of other business. The mail had been neatly stacked. The boxes were alongside the back wall, separated by orange and yellow markers that stood out on the cubicles. He picked up a handful of brochures about "how to get moving in the right direction," a ream of typing paper, and a tape measure. He walked up to the counter, put them down, walked back toward the numbers.

"Nothing but a bunch of junk mail here," he said, turning to me with his lips moving a little. "Do you still want it?"

"Yes, sir."

He breathed hard, as if it was killing him to wait on me. He coughed before walking back to the counter. His eyebrows were connected in the middle, just above the bone in his nose.

"Here you are, missy," he said, slowly passing it to me with the same rigid, teach-you-a-lesson sarcasm in his voice.

I gave it to Daddy through the passenger-side window. He quickly went through it and told me to "just come on and get in the car."

"Goddamn," he said, rubbing his head, "he didn't have no money for me?"

"No, sir," I said, buckling down.

I couldn't ask Mr. Diamond for something he never would have given my daddy in the first place. I had to lie. The lie was how we survived, learning the lie and becoming familiar with it. There was no other way.

"I told you," said Mama.

"Leave it alone, Faye," he said.

She started the car. As she put it in reverse, Willie peeked out from the side of the post office, turning his large eyes at me. I smiled at him, thinking about those words he said to me that day after school. I hadn't really thought of them much after that day, but his presence brought them back to me. He seemed confused by what he was to do in return. He just stood there with that scar going over the tip of his ear, shining in its own ray, thick and maneuvered. The doctors went in there and fucked something up. I heard that his brain had worked a little bit after the windshield cracked his head open, before the doctors went in there and changed him. He stood there, tall and strong, with his face lying flat on the side of the building.

"Remind me to tell your mama to stop by the store," said Daddy, turning his head sideways so I could hear him clearly. "I gotta get Sugar some cigarettes."

"I will."

"Now, Chevrolet," said Mama, interrupting, "you know they ain't gone let you take no smokes in that place. Is you crazy? Last time we went in there, they checked us for fleas."

"Aw, baby," said Daddy, "them guards just as ol' and senile as dirt. Besides, I don't believe they gone do too much checking today."

"How you figure?" she asked.

"The good Lawd say so."

"Since when you know anything 'bout 'the good Lawd'?" asked Mama.

"Since I learned the Way," he said.

She huffed at him, flashing a hand to him as if he bothered her.

We were leaving Pyke County. The people were outside sweeping the dust from their porches, watering their flowers to keep them from drying out in the coming of summer. The word had gotten out that we were going to visit my uncle. I felt it from the old men hanging around in their front yards, watching the car go up the road as we drove by.

"It's gonna be a hot one," said Mama, merging into the interstate traffic. "I can feel it."

"If it's any hotter than last summer," said Daddy, "we gone all burn in hell."

He pulled a cigar from his shirt pocket and put it in his mouth, then struck a match on his jeans. A thick cloud of smoke arose throughout the car. It smelled like hickory. My stomach was weak from it. I rolled my window down and watched the smoke fade into his Afro, around his neckline.

"Chevrolet," said Mama, fanning Daddy's cigar fumes, "I wish you wouldn't smoke so much."

"I got problems."

"Hell," she said, "we all do."

"I ain't hurting nobody, Faye," he said.

"Lawd," she said, turning the mirror sideways, to the left, the right, until she had fixed it on the cars behind us, "seem like forever since I last saw Sugar."

She was nervous. The thought of the drive had done something to her. A country girl leaving the only place that had been home to go into the city. Anything outside the limits of Pyke County was the city to her. She had been up all night praying for God knows what, pacing the hallway in front of my door, with her arms in a circle, looking up at Him through the roof of the house, to the sky.

"He taught you how to talk, Maddy," said Daddy, raising his voice a little at the end of the line. "You know that?"

"I never heard of it," I said.

"Yeah," he said, "your mama had been up all night trying to get you to open your mouth. But Sugar . . . Sugar was a natural. He didn't know that you didn't like your ribs tickled. He put his hand on you, the next thing we know, your first word come out: 'stop.'"

His cheeks thickened on the sides of his face. He smiled high. The cigar hung from his lips. He rolled his window down a little more, and I smelled the smoke on his breath. He kept talking to me, with the words fading from his mouth, into the wind.

"Did you hear me, Maddy?"

"Yes, sir," I said, "I heard you."

My period had come down. I spent the first day soaking in the tub, watching the water turn a scarlet red when the blood drained.

"Don't let your daddy forget those cigarettes, Maddy," Mama said, snickering at Daddy.

"I won't, Ma."

The flesh hung from her arms, jiggling each time the road got rough. She looked over at Daddy to see if he saw that it was still moving, long after the bump. She wanted to change that part of herself. She thought she had become larger over the years. She was afraid that Daddy noticed the extra weight, the loose skin on her arms. That he would leave her because her arms had grown heavy, loose when she hit a bump in the road.

"Lawd help," said Mama.

We were going to see a rapist. I read it in her eyes. She peered over at Daddy. He kept his eyes off the road and was now looking up at the sky for that dead man she saw in the clouds. She took one hand off the wheel and watched him. Her fingers were light on the back of his neck. One stroke to his backbone. A thin, delicate stroke alongside the carrot-orange hairs on the nape of his spine. He felt her there as she rested her arm on the back of the front seat and played with him. She had stood beside him through the rape, the arm cutting (bathing him twice a day in turpentine and herbs), the fucking of her sister, the whispers, the snoring, the whores.

The wind picked up the sleeve of his missing arm. It flapped and made a noise much like that of an old maid stepping off the front porch to stretch the quilt over the clothesline, using the broom to beat the dust out of it. That loose octopused nub flapped in the rough air and hung into a fistful of fat, an enlarged shape of a snail moving up the side of his shoulder.

"You send that letter to the warden like I tol' you?" he asked.

"Chevrolet," said Mama, "you know better. 'Course I sent it."

He looked at her with aggravation. "All right."

He lifted his head from the seat in midair and looked at her. He wanted her to say it without his having to ask. Why had she made him ask? Didn't she know how much it bothered him to be reminded of his illiteracy? Sure enough, she had helped him get along, but there were times when she hurt him, made him feel that his dependence on her validated him. Every word came from her or me, carefully attended by some arrogance she had acquired, some air of dictatorship, because she held his vocabulary in her hands, as stiff and forward as an iron hoe going into a row of untouched earth.

She felt him staring at her. "What?" she said. "What did I do?"

He rested his head back on the seat, sideways. "Nothing," he said.

And I saw his face in the mirror, subconsciously thinking about the long drive, the changed wife he had married once, when he was able to hold her in his arms with both hands.

A booth was just ahead of us. A red-haired man looked out from the box-shaped window and opened a book that appeared to be lying on the counter in front of him. He was in uniform, his round, motionless face taking up the limited space around him.

Daddy began to reach in his back pocket to search for the Mississippi identification card that the state had given him on account of his driving around a sick woman, my grandmother, when they were on good terms. Instead, the picture of me that he cherished fell out. He looked at it and smiled before finding the card behind it.

The red-haired guard looked at Mama. "How many?" he asked.

"Three," said Mama.

"Your name on the list?" he asked.

She paused and looked at Daddy, some part of her hoping that she had planned everything out all right. "Yes, sir."

"Give 'em to me," he said.

While calling out the names, she suddenly appeared nervous. Was he going to ask her what the prisoner had done? If he was as violent as the other numbers? He looked at her, then at Daddy, before asking for identification. Mama gave it to him.

He scrolled down the pages of the book. "The name?" he asked.

"Sugar," she said. "'Scuse me, mister. I mean Paul Ray Dangerfield."

The engine was hot from the drive. The fumes rose from the hood of the car, going upward into the air around us. The guard pulled his finger back from the catalog of numbers.

"Three up!" he said, holding up a walkie-talkie.

The prison was a cold place. There was razored barbwire aligning the entrance, coiled into circular rows atop an iron fence. The heat rose from the concrete. And the clouds were not lazy anymore. They had dropped off a while back, the paleness of them breaking up into an imperfect motion.

Mama kept the cards in her pocket, nervously hanging on to Daddy's arm. Before leaving the house, she had asked me to help pull her panties up on her. She said that going to a lockup was not the same as sitting house. You had to wear an extra pair of panties underneath your stockings so the numbers wouldn't smell your private parts. They had kept themselves busy dreaming about the hairs of a woman's vagina, locating the spot below her navel and putting their fingers in it. When I was done helping her, she pushed me into my room and told me to do the same.

Another guard walked up to us. He patted Daddy down, then Mama and me. He opened the door, and the smell of urine emerged. Toward a distant corridor, a man yelled out a collection of words that Mama told me never to repeat. I wanted to trail the echo of his voice, find him, and ask him what he was doing there. From the moment you enter the place, you are no longer human. There is a lump in your throat the size of a brick wall. It blocks the uprising of saliva, and you will feel it sliding back through the canal of your esophagus, coming up only to be cut off by fear. You want to know many things. This is the place where they keep the punished, the dead, the dying.

We opened a steel door the color of a newly hatched yard egg. There were many people seated in tin chairs, a line of old ladies, men, fathers, uncles, cousins, and mothers waiting their turn.

The energy of the wait yawned throughout the rectangular room. There were two small windows, one to the right of the building, another in back. The smell of ammonia had grown thicker. The visitors looked at us and returned to their activities. There was a seat between a woman and a little boy that hadn't been taken. Mama took it and pointed to two other seats alongside a distant row. I took Daddy's hand and waited beside him.

A pregnant woman sat next to me. Her face was flat, as if she had been thrown from a car and it had crushed the bones. She dug into the mouth of her purse and pulled out a set of sketches. She looked at them with a cunning smile, hiding them behind her hands. When she exposed one of them, I saw a baby caught in the tubes. The baby was a girl. Her eyes were closed, and the tubes of her mother's intestines were wrapped around her throat. I had felt this way before. There were times when I dreamt of this: a baby wrapped in the tubes of her mother's stomach. Because something had happened to me that I could not explain: there was only the scent of milk on my breath, from a distant breast, from a woman other than my own mother—for I could not have imagined it otherwise. The pregnant woman began to rub her belly. The baby was inside her stomach, she said, kicking her for not feeding him this morning. "That's what he do," she said, talking to the cat-eyed boy beside her. "He got his daddy in 'im."

I thought of how very innocent Willie was: his mother tucking him in her blouse on the drive, until his lips were fixed on her nipple. And his father beside her—the three of them rising in midair, crashing through the windshield, into the trees. And the coroner telling Mama that the mother's hands were permanently cradled because at the end of her life she had taken a woman's instincts into the ground with her.

The pregnant woman pulled her shirt out of her pants and sighed. As it slowly began to come up, I saw the long dark line on her belly, the stretch marks spreading on the brink of her flesh like cobwebs. What sound was made when doctors cut a woman from the stomach? Was it the sound of a knife going into a garden watermelon, sharp?

The words came out so very quickly. "Can I touch your stomach?" I asked.

The activities of the visitors seemed to come to a pause. None of them looked directly at me, except for Mama. Her eyes were laced with embarrassment. Not Daddy's. He said nothing.

"Go 'head," said the pregnant woman. "I don't mind."

She took my hands and pressed them on the side of her belly. The baby was warm inside of her. Her hands were cold, but the fetus had heated up her ovaries and sent a flame throughout her swollen body. "Feel 'im kicking?" she asked.

"A little," I said, unsure of whether it was the baby or her hunger that I felt.

She changed the positioning of my hands. "What about now?"

I smiled. "I can't feel him at all now."

"He gone back to sleep," she said. "He mad."

She pulled her shirt back down and answered a question set to her by another pregnant woman on the back row. "Nine months," she told her. "Big, huh?"

They began to converse back and forth. She was at a prison in her ninth month, a baby she had carried for almost an entire year. Why spend it here? I thought. Especially when those months would never count. And she'd have to use her fingers to tell people how old he was.

"I'm just starting out," said the other pregnant woman. "This thing got me all swole up!"

The metal door opened. A guard came out and stood next to it, his arms beside him. The two pregnant women stopped talking. The nine-month one held the cat-eyed boy's hand beside her. It was their turn to go. She reached behind her for the backrest and pushed herself up from the chair. She walked toward the door, her crushed face poignant.

She coughed.

And I looked on the floor for her baby to fall out.

* * *

I had fallen asleep on Daddy's shoulder when the buzz of the metal door woke me. It was a guard leading Mama to the other side. "Can I go, Daddy?"

"No," he said, "wait with me."

The nerves in his nub circulated from his heart to his chest, his shoulders, up to his neck. He had worn a pin-striped oxford. The smell of Mama's perfume was saturated inside the fabric. Her life depended on cutting the long arms out of it and sewing the sleeve just below his nub so no one could see how far the blade had cut him. Although it did not matter to him, he loved her for it. He loved the way she folded her arms when something puzzled her, pressed the babies' bottoms with her hands to see if they were wet. Deep down inside, he loved her because he could not completely change her.

The noises in the prison were worse than thunder passing through a dark cloud. The ticking of something hard on the metal bars, men yelling out to the cart driver for a trade, the wheels of the cart slowly halting at each cell to pass out the trays of food.

A woman carrying a toddler on her hip came and sat next to me. She flopped him down on her lap and rubbed the back of her neck, looking through her purse for something familiar to give her attention to. The toddler started to cry. His hollering vibrated through the walls. The push cart stopped for a second. Then the toddler, looking around, pushed his mother in the chest with his fat fingers. "All right, now!" she said, flipping him over on her lap to remove the heavy diaper from his bottom. She held his feet closely together. Daddy turned his head.

"He too big for diapers," said the woman, talking to me with her mind on her work. "But I work late. Ain't got time to potty-train. He gone learn like his pappy learned." She smiled. "Pull it out and go!"

A few visitors laughed. But Daddy seemed upset with her. She sensed his eyes on her. She was a big woman like Mama. Her face was not flat but round. The weight of her body made her tired. Her words were shifted, each of them growing harder to pronounce as it emerged from her chest, asthmatic-like. She didn't care that Daddy watched her. People had probably been staring at her all of her life. "What you want?" she asked Daddy.

At the same time, she pulled the toddler back to her bosom.

Daddy said nothing. A woman hadn't talked to him that way since my grandmother died. He pretended not to hear her and watched as a muscular-bodied man put his face to the rectangular window. His neck, the dimensions of his head were wide.

A guard walked up behind him, calling out his number. He turned around, and the shackles on his feet and hands added to the thunder of noises. There was a commotion. One, two guards running toward the prisoner, rushing him. "'Ey!" said the number. "'Ey, you motherfuckers! Get off me! 'Ey!"

Even the toddler stopped crying. More guards came to keep him quiet. A man in prescription glasses lifted a hypodermic needle through the small window. The prisoner called out, "'Ey!" Last I heard were the shackles rattling on the floor carrying deadweight.

The woman beside me picked up her purse. "There go my visit," she said. The toddler was on her hip again. She walked up to the rectangular window and shook her head. "When we get back home," she said, looking at the toddler, "we gonna find you a new pappy!"

She walked away. And there, where her feet had once rested on the cold floor, was a picture of *Jesus*, lying on His side, His penis covered by a loincloth. Jesus was a man, indeed.

The nine-month woman came back, holding the cat-eyed boy's hand. She looked on the floor for the picture.

"Here it is," I said, passing it to her.

She looked at it and shook her head. "That's how He lay when the hole in His side be hurtin' 'im," she said, leaving the prison.

Mama had returned from her visit with Uncle Sugar. She was beginning to change her mind. Her hands were around her throat gently. The other visitors were listening. A couple of them laughed.

Daddy kneeled beside her. "We done come all this way," he whispered.

He finally calmed her down and convinced her to let me go. She turned and looked at me. "Come here," she said, wrapping her hands around my strong face. Then she turned away from me. "Now, go."

And I went, holding on to Daddy's good arm. The buzzer sounded as the door locked behind us. We were led to a row of cubicles. The windows were much smaller now, tubular and thin. And underneath their shapes was a bracket of holes where the visitors put their mouths up close to talk. An old woman was in the first cubicle, her throat stretched up toward the holes, telling a number that she wanted him to cut his beard. The judge would think that he was some kind of animal with uncut hair on his face. Another woman, middle-aged, lowered her head, the eyes of her number on the other side watery. A man, his hands flat on the counter, praying for *Jesus* to let his son remain untouched. Another one, in a wheelchair, a plastic tube going through his nose, as if he had swallowed ammonia. His hands were flattened clear up to the knuckles, his spine crushed at the neck, the thin unmoving legs. Finally, I recognized the eyes that had been hanging over Mama's bedpost in an oval locket.

Daddy sat down, my hands on his shoulders. Uncle Sugar didn't have the eyes of a rapist. My grandmother had told me many times that the devil had a shadow to his eyes. His were different from the others. They were solid.

For a short while, he and Daddy were quiet, until Uncle Sugar spoke through the triangular holes. "How's it been?"

"All right," said Daddy. "I can't complain."

They were both nervous. The veins in Uncle Sugar's eyes were scarlet red, as if he had been up all night deciding what he was going to say, how he was going to approach the meaning of the letters.

"I'm still a man," said Uncle Sugar.

Daddy lowered his voice. "I know."

"Them niggers on Factory ain't crossin' you, is they?" asked Uncle Sugar.

"Naw, baby," said Daddy. "Ain't no nigger gone punk me."

"Not even Jesus?" asked Uncle Sugar. "You ain't believing them lies, is you?"

"What lies?"

"'Bout him killing a man," said Uncle Sugar. "If you is, you better let go of it. 'Cause Jesus ain't nothing but a feather. They found that nigger in lockdown with a belt around his neck."

Daddy's face was flushed. He had been giving Mama's hard-earned money to a coward. What was he going to do now? The burden of his life had fallen into his lap. He had become the hog that he'd slaughtered.

"Hell naw!" he yelled. "Not even Jesus Sanders."

Uncle Sugar wrestled with some distant thought. He spoke with more depth. "Your house is your nest egg. That's where you lay your head at night," he said. "Don't ever let a motherfucker steal your nest egg!"

They had been apart for some time. But they knew each other. Daddy missing an arm, him missing the set of balls that God had given him. But the similarity of blood was deep inside of them, carrying the lead of a victimized bird in their flesh.

"Don't worry none," said Daddy.

Uncle Sugar moved away from the window. He looked around at the guard behind him, the birthmark that we both shared tattooed between the eyes, a circus elephant. He wore a bright red jumpsuit with the letters MDOC—Mississippi Department of Corrections—stamped on him with a row of numbers beneath it. The men in the cells began to holler, asking the cart driver, other men, for a trade: cigarettes, jungle juice, blow jobs. Their voices rose above the bars of the penitentiary. The metal door opened behind Uncle Sugar and a transvestite walked in. He sat beside him. "Hey lady," said Uncle Sugar.

"Shut up, Sugar," said the transvestite. "You just fuckin' with me."

Uncle Sugar smiled and looked at Daddy for a response.

The guard walked up behind them. Uncle Sugar's eyes were glossy under the fluorescent lightbulbs. The hard walls were bridling him. He wanted to say something. He was in a tough place, a cold place where the lights went out at the same time every night and the sun was hidden behind the hard, yard-egg-colored walls.

His eyes were on me now.

"Don't look at me like that," he said. "I taught you how to open your mouth."

"Good," I said, "now I know how to scream."

His head came crashing down on the counter. Neither Daddy nor I could see him. We waited for him to rise again. The transvestite began to poke at him, laughing. Daddy's shoulders grew tense.

Uncle Sugar began to sigh. When his head came back up to the window, a tear fell from his eyes. "I didn't do it," he said. "Laurel

Pillar had a diamond in her eyes that night. And I didn't put it there."

He stopped for a moment to look at my face. He thought that I was still the one reading the letters.

Daddy's breath fogged up the window.

"Help me get outta here!" said Uncle Sugar.

The transvestite laughed at him. "Yeah, lady," he said. "None of us did it."

The circus elephant changed colors. It was no longer scarlet red but violet, turning up between his eyes in a thick mound of muscle, anger. He threw the chair and began to pound the face of the transvestite. The guard pulled out a baton and began beating them. Other guards came and carried them away, in the exact manner they had carried the other number. And the last we saw of Uncle Sugar was his legs giving out from under him, the shackles on his feet rattling on the hard floors like an innocent man in purgatory.

The wind blew through my hair. I sat in the backseat of the car confused, listening to the wind of the open road. Before long, we were dropping Daddy off at the house and Mama was taking me back to Commitment Road. Once we arrived, she sat in the front yard of Aunt Pip's house with the motor running. And when she drove off past the field, I remembered that I had forgotten to remind Daddy to get the cigarettes.

chapter

ten

Fat had stopped by the house to tell Aunt Pip that the Lord had given her a sign: forty strikes a day on the oak tree would relieve her of the evil done to Justice Bates. This way she could sleep at night. And the devil would leave her alone. She pounded away at the large oak tree in her front yard, counting aloud the number of times she made contact with it.

Aunt Pip was in the bathroom peeing. The house smelled of urine, as she was becoming less willing to travel through the house to use the toilet. She was getting better, but the therapy had made her tired, slow. A metal bedpan, long and horizontal, lay at the side of her bed. It was here where I watched her in the darkness at night, kneeling down with her dress pulled up to her pelvic bone, reaching for the safe space underneath her vagina, waiting for the pee to come down.

"Maddy," she hollered.

I ran to the bathroom. She put my hand on her stomach. "You feel it?" she said.

"No," I said. "I don't feel a thing."

She pushed my hand away and reached for it again, going deeper to the left, toward the lung. "It's sharp," she said, "like a butcher knife or something other."

I shook my head.

"Sometimes," she said softly, "it feel like Adam and Eve are plucking away at my insides with a long-handled spoon."

She was touching the orange penis of the magnolia as it found its way through the cycle of air and penetrated her in her sleep. This was not unusual. She had begun to find other things to locate, other matters of buried illnesses that she felt remained hidden, locked up in a burrow of disease. "There it is again!" she yelled.

I was angry with her. Why couldn't she have been happy that her hair was growing back? What happened to the woman I remembered, the fight in her? To sit and watch her that way, speaking until her throat grew hoarse, rubbing the fabric of the curtains until the edges began to fray. One good day. One bad day. I never knew which came first, only when the sun came up.

"It's the carrots from the soup," I told her.

This relaxed her. She let out a full breath and patted her chest. "Yeah," she said, "the soup."

I followed her into the main room. She picked up the metal bedpan and smelled it. Every time she peed, it was me who emptied it. But it was never clean enough. The scent of ammonia found its way into her nostrils. "Take it out into the yard and let it air out," she said.

The bedpan was cold. I looked at my reflection. My face was loose, the nose in a remote corner, the eyes broken up like someone had cut them out and pasted them to a flat surface, the mouth almost unnoticeable, shapeless.

I walked around the side of the house. A bucket of rainwater lay still. And before anything happened, Aunt Pip spoke to me from the curtains. "Not there," she said, "in the forest."

A small stain the size of an erasure drifted through her gown. Had it not been so noticeable, so important, I would have taken it for granted. A small thing to a curious eye.

My eyes hungered for anything that the world neglected. Like the double-jointed arms of the Mr. Goodbar bully. I had, many times, thought of how I could sneak up behind him and pop his arm from the elbow, pausing the ticking clock in his chest.

Fat had long made her fortieth strike. She was walking on the other side of the trees. Her feet made the routine of fetching a pot of hot water from the stove, stepping from the porch, and following her already beaten path to the tub that sat on the side of her house. After pouring the first pot, she walked back up the steps of her front porch and came out with a second that had lain on the eye of the stove, waiting for her to reach for it. She added this one to the first. Upon which I heard the sound of the pipes behind her house, her hand twisting the star-shaped handle and pulling the rubber hosepipe from under the fragile house.

She was naked by this time. Through the trees, she looked like a giant bear, her steps forcing the ground before her to succumb to her weight. There she was. Her large head passing between the pine, her face going upward and away from the field where Daddy and the white men left hours before to wait for a heavy rain to lift the stalks of corn from the earth.

"Ouch!" yelled Fat.

Then the pipes under the house started whistling again. Her mountainous body leaned toward the temperature of the tub. She was not pleased and began to press her thumb on the mouth of the sprouting hosepipe. Where had I imagined that sound?

I stood in the middle of the forest, looking back at where I had first brushed a branch from my path. And it came to me, a light of laughter. It was the children I imagined. The boy and girl over the mantel flinching from the mouth of the hosepipe. Many times I had overlooked them, passed their faces and judged them as ordinary misplacements.

Fat settled in the tub. She wrung a pink towel out in her hands, letting it slide over the thick piece of meat between her legs. She pulled the towel toward her and smelled it before dipping it back into the water, rubbing behind her ears. Her back was in loaves from behind. Three layers of meat that hung over the porcelain like the fresh slaying of cattle.

"New Orleans," she said, laughing.

My foot got caught in a briar patch. It was then that I realized I'd left the bedpan far behind, seeing the metal in some uncomfortable position of the woods, the paleness of the sky beaming around it. I slowly pinched the spikes of briars at my ankles. I untangled them and discovered a thin line of clotted blood going up my leg, resembling the perforated edge of a sharp instrument.

Fat was still laughing alone.

It seemed she wanted to be disturbed, almost waited for someone to walk up behind her and put his hand under the body of warm water and touch her life. That's where it was indeed. Everything. The blood of her husband. The intimate hairs plucked from her vagina by the age of water, the alphabets. Perhaps even the whistle of the star-shaped handle flooding the rubber hosepipe to intimidate her by force.

I left the bedpan in the woods and returned to Aunt Pip. She was sitting up with a postage stamp in her hands—the American flag. I noticed an opened letter beside her; it was from the doctors in Jackson, the machinists.

"Go on up to Fat's," she said, her head turned, frozen like the mouth of the ceramic doll. "She get lonely this time o' day."

* * *

The sky was bare. Only a blue that came and went upon the stretch of the land. As I walked toward the house, I smelled the soap from Fat's inner thigh. It was a scent that rose into the air like a woman beater after the curtains went down.

She was there in the porcelain tub yet pushing the pink towel between her legs. The bathwater moved over the curves of her skin. Her breasts sagged to her waist, full breasts that could have covered the earth. She looked up at me, startled.

"Child," she said, "you walking up in this yard like you read the Bible on your back."

"Huh?" I turned away from her breasts.

"You know what they say," she said. "If you read the Bible on your back, you got nerve."

The caterpillars were falling on the ground. They had eaten holes in the hanging tree leaves. Tiny holes that were brown around the edges.

"If you say so," I said.

"What wind blew you this way?" She sat up with her back against the tub and draped the pink towel over its border, her nipples hardened. I remembered the pictures in the National Geographic, how the babies' lips curved outward with those same hardened nipples in their mouths.

"Aunt Pip sent me to keep you company."

"I'll be," she said, smiling. Her face was in the clouds, her nipples swelling away from the flesh of her breasts. "I love her for it."

The green caterpillars glided across the aluminum like the lizard that found its way on Aunt Pip's window. Green and unaware of its greenness.

She wiped her face. "That Collins boy ain't seen you nekked yet, is he?"

"No."

"Good," she said, lifting her arms from the water and holding them out to me. "Come here."

I walked over to her, my white dress about me.

"Where this come from?" she asked.

"Mama made it for me."

She paused and pulled the dress up to my waist. "Lawd, Jesus," she said, laughing. "This child got on white underclothes."

"What's wrong with that?" I asked.

"It's a sin to be that close to yourself," she said. "You 'posed to wear black drawers to keep them eyes off o' you. You letting the whole world in your business."

Her words were strong as she pushed me away from her and further into the green. I couldn't imagine this woman saving letters from a dead man.

"Get me some more hot water from the house," she said.

The elastic in my panties was wet from her fingertips. I walked backward, watching her wipe the thick bush between her legs; it looked like a bird's nest when she lifted her bottom out of the water.

She trusted me enough to go inside. But I was afraid to touch anything, because it would come up later. If something was missing or fucked with, she would blame me. I knew because I had seen the distrust between *us*. I heard the rumors about black women who stabbed their sisters because they didn't trust them with their men. About high-class Mississippi niggers who went to prison for killing a brother, a daddy, an uncle, a best friend for hanging around their house too long. My grandmother used to read the obituaries of the dead. "It's the heat, baby," she'd say. "It's Mississippi."

The house felt cold. I didn't know if it was because of the shade trees hanging over the house or that she lived alone. Cold like Miss Hattie Mae's house after her husband had died. Two widows. Two dead husbands. There was a drawing of *Jesus* on the refrigerator.

She had used a red Crayola to lay His body flat on the paper. Her hands were heavy, the red sunken into the paper where the thorns stuck out of His head. She had pinned Him down with a magnet that read: "A lonely bitch is the only fool I know."

The pot was boiling over on the stove, the handle hot. I opened the drawers and the cupboards, searching for something to lift it with. She had boxes and boxes of powdered milk. Other than that, the kitchen was empty. Nothing of the good in her life. Just that one picture of *Jesus* pinned to the refrigerator and trails of powdered milk pressed across the floor and the smell of juniper floating through the house.

"The rag's over the oven," she yelled.

When I made it back to the tub, she lifted her fingers again, saying: "Pour it on in here, girl. Don't be scared."

"I don't wanna burn you," I said.

"It's all right," she said, staring through my white dress with a look of curiosity. "You done had your period yet?"

"Yes, ma'am."

"How old?" She signaled for me to stop pouring. I put the pot down on the grass and stepped back.

"I don't know." I grew angry with her. But it was rude to walk off from a Negro in Mississippi. She would have slapped the shit out of me for leaving her there in the middle of a question.

"Well"—she laughed, her wisdom teeth missing—"you best stay away from that Collins boy. Men know the smell o' blood."

Black women in Pyke County believed that once a girl's period came on, she was getting too grown for her body. And that men could tell her pores were open, like pregnant women who weren't allowed in the cornfield because the snakes could smell their breast milk, strangle them.

Fat sat up in the tub. "You ever seen a man before?"

"My daddy."

She shook her head. "No, child. A man besides your daddy. A naked man."

"In the Bible."

"Did he move when you touched him?" she asked, her eyes larger this time.

"No."

"Well," she said, "that's not the kind o' man I'm talking about." She sank back down into the tub, her chin on the edge of the water. "I met one man in my life who came this close to *Jesus*." She held her thumb and index finger an inch apart.

Justice Bates. A hanged man. A dead man. She loved him still, her eyes all lit up, her cheeks rising into a mountain.

The breath from Fat's stomach rippled the water. "I know they call me crazy," she said. "But I don't care. Don't nobody know but *Jesus*."

She crossed her legs and stretched them across the side of the tub to support herself. There were spiders on her thighs—cobwebs and spiders that went up from the fur between her legs, up to her navel in a winding narration. The cobwebs were lighter than her skin, leaving the hole in her navel the shape of an unpicked Afro.

"How come you stay locked up at Pip's all the time?" She rose from the water and looked up at the caterpillars, turning the tub over on the ground. The inside was dark, sooty.

"I want to ask you something," I said.

She stood over the tub, walking the bottom of the porcelain with her fingertips. "All right," she said.

"What'd you do with him?"

Her thoughts lifted her face to the early beginnings of the afternoon. "I burned him," she said, "so I know what it feel like to be naked with him again."

Before I knew it, she was turning the corner of the house, beckoning me to follow, her face on a fixed gaze of nostalgia.

Once inside, she sprinkled baby powder on her breasts. It came out in a large cloud. She left the room for a second and returned with a pair of panties in her hands, lowering them before pulling them up, over her thighs. "I know what you did at the church," she said. "You gotta be the craziest cow I know to do some shit like that."

She walked back down the hall, shortly thereafter shuffling through the drawers. The tiny green lamp next to the velvet couch was shifting forward, unbalanced. Her powdered footprints made tracks across the floor; the pattern of her perfectly round toes like an enlarged grain of sugar.

"I have to go," I said.

"Where's you running off to?" Her voice grew heavy. She came from the room dressed in a thin-laced gown, holding up a joint.

"Aunt Pip's probably waiting on me," I said, watching her light the joint as she sat on the velvet couch.

She pulled me close to her, saying: "Close your eyes."

"What for?"

"Just close 'em!"

I did. The heat from her body made me nervous as she blew smoke into my nostrils. I thought I'd never stop coughing. When I opened my eyes again, she was rolling across the wooden floor with her hands on her belly.

"I'm leaving," I said.

"Fat say try," she said. "Go on. Try!"

The faucet dripped into a loud, solid thump in the hollow sink. It grew louder as I looked at her on the floor like that, laughing at me and running her fingers over the hairs in her head. She had been burned beneath her arms.

"What you laughing at?" I asked, unable to stand up.

I hated her for not tightening the faucet. My head was about to float away from my body. Nothing but the sound of that water pounding deeper into my scalp, the hellish laughter that came from Fat, Moses above me—holding the Ten Commandments.

"It won't hurt you," said Fat, sitting on the velvet couch now with her shoulders calming down from the laughter.

I reached for her hair, but the closer I got, the more her head leaned forward. She pulled a small picture from the cushions, stared at it, and put it back.

I lay down on the velvet, my head spinning. "You ever mind what they say?" I asked.

"Nope," she said.

Immediately, she jumped off the couch, her large, snail-shaped body making its way to the mailbox. She grabbed the envelope and ran back toward the house with the letter in her hands. Her pace picked up, the closer she got to the front porch. I wanted to take her breasts in my hands and laugh about the largeness of them.

"I knew he'd write," she said. "It's that time of the week."

She pulled hard on the joint until the tip of it turned a bright orange. Then she opened the envelope, shriveling the white paper on the floor.

"Read it," I said.

The handwriting was childlike, familiar. "I'm too excited," she said, as if it was the first she'd ever gotten. "You read it."

"I can't."

Everything was blurry: the images strewn together, the faucet thundering into an outburst every second, her hips in that gown, my wanting to put her breasts in my hands to let one of those doctors in Jackson, Mississippi, check them for cancer.

"I'll read it myself, then!" she yelled.

I regretted not hearing the words or listening to her speak them. All I remember is the smell of her fur when she walked back and forth on the floorboards. The faucet, the heat rising up from the lightbulb, the machines, Mama ironing out the wrinkles in Daddy's clothes, Billie Holiday's shoulders, the circumference of a circle, Auschwitz, Willie Patterson, death, my death, Landy Collins, the faucet, the sound of a woman's voice, Hitler, so many other things that I could not remember to save my life.

The sun was going down over the field.

"I'm gonna marry Landy Collins one day," I said.

Fat turned to me, her head sideways. "You can't marry him."

"Why not?"

"'Cause," she said, "that nigger got a ol' lady in New Orleans."

"That's the biggest lie I ever heard."

"That's what I hear tell," she said, blowing the smoke from her lungs. "He like 'em young."

I laughed.

"I hear she pregnant for him too!" said Fat.

I couldn't do a damn thing about it. The velvet was getting cold, my body was going numb. And Fat's constant reading of the letter was putting me to sleep, her hand occasionally digging back into the couch to pull something out, hide it again.

chapter
eleven

The sound of the chain saw ricocheted off the bark of the trees. Landy Collins had been in the forest all afternoon, cutting down a row of pine trees for the next death. Occasionally, he would stop working, as if listening to Fat count aloud the number of times she'd struck the large oak.

I was sitting on the front porch when Aunt Pip came out to join me. She sat on the steps of the house with her head up, stretching her arms out in front of her, then on her stomach. "I got the world in there," she said.

She wore her blond wig and a fake diamond from her jewelry box. An ant began to crawl up the side of her foot; she killed it. She then opened her gown and slid her fingers down over the lizard-shaped scar, the heat climbing around it. Her eyes were closed now, the occasional wind whistling around the corners of the house. The diamond had begun to make a lump through her gown; she kept her hand there over the lizard's backbone.

She laughed out loud, her voice like a mountain. "You think Eve told Adam what to do?" She did not wait for an answer; her laughter stopping now, controlled. "I had a dream I swallowed the bastard."

"Adam?"

Her face was calm.

"Yeah," she said, "I ate my Father."

She turned around and reached for my hands, as she had the morning she vomited the things from her stomach into the toilet. "I know," she said. "It ain't the soup carrots. It's my Father. He in there somewhere fooling around with me."

"Don't keep things from me," I said, moving to the edge of the porch.

She listened as the chain saw got going again. "Hear that?" she asked, making fists of her hands. "That's what it be like all the time. Cutting at you from the bone. Chipping away at you. Chipping away at you."

"Everyone keeps things," I said. "Nobody gives anything away."

Her voice fell into a whisper: "Except green things." Her hand was away from her breast. "Don't take nothing green from nobody. Green things die."

She was not demented. For when I watched her bathe herself, her chin was still above the water. I heard that a demented woman practiced drowning. She forced her head under the water and waited for her nostrils to fill up, and when she came up coughing, she knew what it was to be yet alive.

"My titty still sick, Maddy," said Aunt Pip.

I turned around to face her. There was no sadness about her. "What are you telling me?"

"I'm telling you that I ate my Father," she said. "I opened my mouth and let the sins of the world in my body and even He couldn't fix it. And now I'm paying for it."

The little bit of hair that had grown back would be lost again. She would soon find herself facing the machine once more, the compressor coming down on her breast, the doctors using their tools to radiate it.

"I'm going to the piano room," she said.

She got up to go back inside the house. She was naked underneath her gown. The split between her thighs thickened as it went inside her body like a lump of earth. Like mine before the hair grew on it.

I could hear Fat sweeping the dust from her front porch. Her screen door slammed against the boards of the house each time she went inside to get something. I pictured her resting on the wooden pillars of her house, as if she knew the maximum amount of strain to put on them.

Landy Collins was out there in the woods, debating the age of the trees, how far the blade would go. I called out to him.

"Landy," I said. The sound of my voice echoed through the forest. I discovered a cricket propped up on its hind legs. I picked it up between my fingers and watched the torso against the shade of my brown penny loafers. The cricket fought to get away from me.

"Maddy?" asked Landy, calling out from his work.

I put the restless cricket back on the ground and stood there, watching it blend back into the leaves of the forest. "Here I am."

He was deep in the woods with his hands on his hips, as he stood spread-eagled looking up into the hovering sky. As I approached him, I noticed his shoulders stretching out the blood in his arms.

"I would've stopped by," he said, "but it was nice and early when I drove up, and I didn't wanna disturb you and Miss Pip."

"No matter."

He smiled with the shine of goat's milk in his teeth. His head moved forward, out into the air with his skin still dry from the blinding heat. He began to lean down over a tree that had already been cut down. The rings were scarlet red, fresh. He traced the years of the tree with his thick fingers and looked up toward the sky, one eye closed.

"What sent you this way?" he said, propping his foot up on the bark of the tree. His shirt was thrown on the earth; the hair on his chest formed a tornado, the tail of it hidden inside his navel, picking up below his abdomen.

"Nothing," I said.

He laughed. "Is that what you think?" he said, his hands beside him.

I envisioned myself parting the hairs of his head and sniffing them. I had never seen a man so strong: fingers built like commandments, the details of his shoulders parallel to something unnamed, pressed to the collarbone, strict.

"I wish I owned the world," I whispered.

His response was quick, as if the bones of an oyster were closing in on his lungs: "No, you don't," he said. "The man who owns the world owns all the trouble in it."

Without thinking, without any reason at all, I walked up to him and pulled my dress down from the shoulders. No one had truly touched me. "Trouble?" I said.

He began to laugh again, before a shadow suddenly appeared in his eyes. He took my hair in his hands and coiled it around his fingertips. "This what you come out here for?" he asked. "To get yourself in trouble?"

"I don't know."

He began to sweat now. The liquid was leaving his forehead, crawling down over the tip of his wide, flat nostrils. "I could hurt you," he said.

He let my hair go and turned his back to me.

"But you wouldn't," I said.

The sky began to remove itself. No blue and no God.

Landy Collins walked up to me, pulling the straps back over my shoulders. "You don't want what you ask me for," he said.

"But you touched my feet," I said.

"Yeah," he said, "'cause I know the road you on."

He moved around, his muscles moving forward. "I make boxes for little girls like you," he said. "Is that what you want? You want me to make a box for you?"

I grew nervous. "No."

"If you trying to get saved," he said, "you go to *Jesus*. I already got one belly pushed up."

He picked up the chain saw again, turning in the direction of a grown pine tree. The earth was silent. The crickets were no longer chirping. And Fat had slammed the door of her house long ago. I was alone in the world.

As I began to walk away, Landy Collins, without ever turning around, said to me: "Did she ever tell you what they call me?"

"Who?" I asked.

"Fat," he said.

"No."

He then turned around, smiling. "They call me the teaser."

The chain saw began to sound again. And the sun beamed down through the trees, creating a sphere of light that aligned itself in a shadow, peering heavily upon the branches.

chapter
twelve

Aunt Pip had been asleep all day. It was midnight when she finally woke up. She stood in the front door for a moment, her hair covered in a sheet of yellow fabric. The dim light behind her lit up her gown where her legs were poised in a straight line. She closed her eyes and sighed before coming out to sit beside me on the steps, a place we had grown used to.

"Did it rain?" she asked, with one hand over my shoulder.

I felt a pulsating vein in her wrists. This was her living blood, running up through her body in an ordinary pattern. Common, like the laughter of children: a thing of its own dependence.

I looked away from her. The moon was full. It was high above the magnolias, raised in a perfect circle. "It rained a little while," I said.

She leaned back on the porch, her elbows flat on the boards. Slowly, she began to pull her gown up where a row of bobby pins had bordered the elastic in her panties. She removed the yellow fabric from her head, the blond wig exposed. The hair fell; she lifted it above her neck to tame it. "I live like an old woman," she said, smiling.

Between the space of our breathing, the whistling leaves of the oak drifted in the night air. The oak stood above the others, muscular and loud. Only this noise overcame us before she spoke under the yellow moonlight.

"Tomorrow," she said, reaching under her arm. "I go back again."

She said these words from her stomach where alphabets came from. Not from her voice but from the pit of her abdomen, where her throat was tall and useful.

"I know," I said.

She stared through the darkness, past the light of the house. With this, she touched the blond wig and put one last pin on the side of her panties, above the others.

"It wasn't this way the first time," she said. "I let them cut me."

"Did it hurt?" I asked.

"It only hurt to wake up," Aunt Pip said, pausing. "That's when the mirrors come down."

How could I have counted every star in the sky that night, the unusually bright one, forming a circle between the others? Was it this way with women? One bright star upon another, each circulating in a pattern of dependence? The gathering of light, one holding the other, in an attitude of sickness, faithful to the earth around it.

The oak whistled louder, although no wind had reached us. Indeed, I had forgotten what it was like to swallow bread during Communion, what it was like to have the taste of Jesus Christ in my mouth, for if His love came in the form of stars, I had missed its glowing altogether.

I was a child of opinion. Every thought created within me, from birth, was like this one bright star, circling the kitchen of my mania, my depression. In this area of consciousness, my house of bereavement, I wondered where Aunt Pip's missing breast was, if it was labeled beside Willie's brain. What did men do with something they knew nothing about? There was no balance for a missing thing. It had all gone to the yellow moon, creating within it a beam of glowing pity.

Aunt Pip began to pace the wooden boards, still looking out into the silent darkness with her eyelids erect. "The first time they took my titty," she said, "I tried to tell your mama. But she wouldn't listen."

"What did she do?"

Aunt Pip turned away from the darkness and touched me. "She pushed me," she said. "She pushed me in the same side where my titty missing." Her voice stopped reaching for a familiar word: "That's what hurt most. She couldn't tell that part o' me was flat."

When the whistling of the wide oak stopped, she looked over at a lantern that had been sitting on the porch since the rain. It appeared to be more than a thing of presence. She stretched her arms out and picked it up. "Look at it," she said.

She sat it back down again and went inside the house. The figure of her waist underneath the gown was disturbing, the shape of her hipbone going upward, linking in the direction of her lungs. She returned with a pair of tweezers and kneeled over the lantern.

"How old is it?" I asked.

She never looked up. Instead, she scraped the mud from the belly of glass. "Since the flood," she said.

When the clay began to break, she picked up the pieces around her and ate them. With each lump, she looked behind her, as if something was there. That was when a more distinct noise came from the woods. The feet came down harder than rain coming from a cloud. There was pressure on the toes.

"You hear that?" I asked.

She smiled. "Yeah," she said, smiling. "When you live on Commitment, you hear everything God made."

The noise grew louder, as if the feet were approaching the porch in the darkness. I pushed myself back against the screen door. "I'm scared."

"Don't be," said Aunt Pip.

She said this so calmly, crushing the red dirt in her fingers and swallowing it. When the sound of the feet stopped, the oak picked up again. One sound to another.

"Ain't you?" I asked.

"Open your mouth," she said fearlessly. She had crushed the red dirt into a fine powder in the palm of her hand. "Taste it."

I did.

This was God. It was different from the cracker of Communion. It tasted of rain. The rain that had fallen off the rooftops of every house in Pyke County had formed a red river of blood. You should have tasted this. I was eating the brightest star in the sky. I was swallowing the taste of God.

"I ain't scared at all," said Aunt Pip, turning her back to me.

She had poured a piece of the earth into my mouth. Without ever realizing it, she had baptized me. She brought the lantern to the house light, as her backbone turned into a shade of blue. When the tweezers were firm in her hands, she twisted the glass from the base and pulled out a tiny piece of paper with the letter "J" written on it.

She stood over me, nursing the paper, flipping it over again and again. She was mesmerized by this object. Nothing alphabetical about it, her stomach rising in the shadow of the light, alive.

"You ever caught the Holy Ghost?" she asked.

"Nome."

She smiled and held the alphabet up toward the sky. "I have," she said. "*Jesus* was inside o' me. And when I went to touch the hole in His side, He disappeared."

"*Jesus* doesn't have a penis," I said.

She laughed with her head pulled back. "Every man's got a burden," she said. "Doesn't matter what name he goes by."

The stars were breaking up. It was possible to move things with the mind. Aunt Pip had done this with her vocabulary. The women were dormant in the sky, aside from their limited fits of laughter, and, in a wave of timeless energy, heard the voice of a sick woman there, on the earth of ignorance, and moved aside to allow her to send forth the powder of dust from her mouth.

"Don't let them take your hair again," I said.

She paused over the thing in her hand. "I have to," she said, one hand over her breast as it hung from her like the octopus of Daddy's missing arm. "I've learned to find myself in other places."

She was undisturbed, her face looking through the screen door, back at the object.

"How will you get there?" I asked.

She walked to the edge of the porch. Her face, from the side, was outlined in the moon. And when the feet came down through the trees again, she whispered, "*Jesus.*"

The next morning, I noticed that Aunt Pip's bed had been fixed. There was no note or sign of her morning activity. She was gone. And Mama was waiting in the front yard with her head to one side, breathing heavily.

chapter
thirteen

Daddy said that his boss, Mr. Sandifer, had a bad case of hay fever; the weather made him irritable. Mama and I were going to the scrap yard to take Daddy some lunch. It was his way of preparing us for the embarrassment he'd suffer from the words of Mr. Sandifer.

Mama pulled into the scrap yard, parking the truck on a patch of broken dust in front of Mr. Sandifer's office, a boarded-up shack with an iron fan in the window. He prided himself in the scrap yard. I'd see him in town buying tools from the hardware store to add to his collection of hammers, nails, wrenches, and other things that came in handy. He peered through the box-shaped window, opening the door with a string of loose keys chiming from his pocket. The earth was a flaming orange, the sun shone at an angle, down over the bridge of his elongated nose.

"How you doing there, Mr. Sandifer?" asked Mama, pulling the side of her dress like a Spanish lover. Her hair had been dyed a funeral dark, the ends split. "I just came over to bring Chevrolet some hot biscuits from the stove."

"I figured that," said Mr. Sandifer. "Come on in." He didn't mean it. I could count on one hand the number of times he'd let us in that place. The last time was in the dead of winter and Mama had locked her keys in the car.

"How's the misses?" asked Mama, putting one hand on her thighbone. The trips to the clothesline hadn't hardened her muscles.

"Doing just fine," he said. His fingers were smooth around the tips. The most work he'd had in them was closing the office door to go home to his wife.

"It's awfully busy this season," said Mama. She had begun to pull the bonnet closer to her scalp, down over her crawling hair. That bad hair that shrank in the rain and the sun drew the grease out of.

"It seems so," he said, looking more like the color of Missouri on Miss Diamond's United States of America map. A pink-flamingo color that curved into the cloth of a pregnant woman's belly.

He shuffled through the papers on his desk, swearing at a fly that buzzed around his head. "Chevrolet," he yelled, "your folks here."

He hated niggers hanging around the place. He had that air about him: the look in his eyes when Mama raised her arms to her hips, the manner in which he covered his mouth thereafter, shifting the mucus to one nostril or another with his smooth hands.

"I'm coming," said Daddy, watching us through the small rectangular window.

"It is time for a break, ain't it Mr. Sandifer?" asked Mama. She had worked hard for white folks all her life. She said that she never ate inside any of their houses because they could see the nigger in her lips. She ate on the back porch with the hounds.

"Yeah," said Mr. Sandifer, looking down at his watch, "I reckon." He walked to the window and tapped the glass to get Daddy's attention again. Daddy looked up at him and nodded his head.

"Mighty kind o' you sir," said Mama.

She pushed me through the back door, where Daddy had begun to put down his tools, stretching his one good arm in the heat. "What you got for me today?" he asked.

Mr. Sandifer's face was disfigured through the screen door as his wrists went up and down, finally resting on a *Life* magazine. He coiled it in his hands and came down on the top of the desk, raising it again and again with an effort to kill the buzzing fly.

Mama patted her chest and waited for Daddy to sit on the edge of the porch. He wiped the sweat from his eyes, his skin reddened in the sun. "I got you some buttermilk biscuits and lemonade," said Mama.

"How's it going, Maddy?" asked Daddy. He looked at me as if embarrassed that he was my father and worked for a white man who talked down to him sometimes.

"All right," I said.

Jesus had cracked his front tooth a couple of weeks ago. Daddy said that Jesus didn't take silver. He took gold. The morning that it happened, Daddy took a slab of hog meat to the pool hall. He called himself making up for a big bet he made with some hustlers from Chicago. He told Jesus that the meat was boneless. But Jesus didn't care. He told Daddy to stay away from Factory Road with that shit. They say that Daddy stood there blessing that hog meat and taking a jar full of silver coins from his pocket. He told Jesus that the meat was good and the silver would last him a long time. They say Daddy took his eyes off Jesus. That's what happened to him.

"Maddy," said Daddy, taking a sip from the glass of lemonade, "you always leaving me. Sometimes I forget what you look like."

Mama interrupted, "Eat up, now, Chevrolet."

"We ain't hurting nobody, baby," said Daddy. He cut the biscuits down the center with his hunting knife. The grease had hardened on the sausage. He scraped it off and slid the knife inside the biscuit. "Just leave it alone, now."

He began to eat the biscuits while looking up at the sky. The clouds were brewing ahead. It was an eerie summer. Things were much different now. He was tired of working for Mr. Sandifer, listening to him talk about how he should have cracked that nigger's skull who chipped his tooth up like that.

Mama felt him drifting away: "We due a storm by Sunday," she said. "Must be why it's been so hot these last few days."

"The world's coming to an end," said Daddy.

A scarecrow hung above the motors in the scrap yard. It was stuffed with straw and erected from a flag pole, hanging in a dead man's clothes—a flannel button-down oxford and overalls. It had been there before I had learned to crawl, lifeless and hitched to a field pulley in the middle of the scrap yard.

"Faye," said Mr. Sandifer, looking out through the screen door, "I need some work done around the house this Sunday, if you don't mind."

Daddy looked up from the biscuits and tried to keep a calm voice about him. A white man had called his wife by her first name. "But I haven't missed a day of work," he said. "I've been here every day for the past couple o' weeks."

Mr. Sandifer opened the screen door and stepped onto the front porch. "I know, Chevrolet," he said. "My Lucille needs some extras done around the house, n' I figured Faye here wouldn't mind doing the work. That is, since I was so kind as to give you that helping o' cornmeal from Pillar's last Thursday."

Mama sensed the tension between them. "Yes, sir," she said, "I don't mind obliging the misses. It's quite all right."

Mr. Sandifer pulled a pear from his pocket and bit into it. His false teeth moved against his gums. "I hope you don't mind, Chevrolet," he said sarcastically.

Daddy lowered his chin. The sweat dripped from the curve in his face onto the biscuits. "No, sir, Mr. Sandifer," he said. "I don't mind."

It was worse than betting on a losing horse. Or the cockfights when the dead rooster was thrown across the fence, his head turned sideways, open-eyed. Or the raccoon-on-the-log when the hound lost and went home with its owner. He gave Jesus everything: his money, Mama's working hands, his manhood, his pride, everything, although it was just as much his fault as Jesus'.

"I don't mind at all," repeated Daddy, putting the biscuits down and turning away. The heat came up from the dust, blending the oil in his hair with the scent of the earth.

"You'd best be getting back to work soon," added Mr. Sandifer.

Mama rubbed her shoulders as Mr. Sandifer went inside. He made her nervous: the thread of her dress pressed deeper into her flesh, flattened out by her rough hands. Because Jesus wouldn't take ham or silver. Only gold.

"We'll be going now," she said. She picked up the basket and kissed Daddy on the brow. She stood there awhile, watching him walk back to an abandoned radiator and pick up one of his tools. "You hear me, Chevrolet?"

He carried my baby picture around in his back pocket so long that it had formed a ragged square patch in his jeans. It was odder than a grown man inside a Radio Flyer for a gambler to care about something, anything. We talked, but I hardly saw that part of him. Only during Easter when he poured the jelly beans out on the kitchen table and gave me all the purple ones.

"No more history in my house, Maddy," he yelled, looking up from the radiator and smiling at me like he did that night he told

me he'd felt his missing arm again, lighting the tip of his cigar and
throwing the match into the air.

"Yes, sir," I said.

I saw the regret in his eyes, the confusion of giving a man his
life.

Mr. Sandifer leaned against the screen door. He raised the delicate bones in his hand to the river of blood in his chest. His eyes
were on the scarecrow, the pulley's force lifting the backbone. The
rare occasions when the rain wilted the haywire and he had to jab
a pitchfork between the cotton in its oxford.

"Sunday be just fine," said Mama. The figs came out in lumps.
This is what bothered her now. Not the work, come Sunday, that
would soak her hair fuzzier than a Georgia peach.

Mr. Sandifer's office door had fallen apart over the years. The
fibers from the screen door frayed outward. "All's fair," he said,
fanning himself with the pages of *Life*.

The truck wouldn't start at first. Mama prayed over the wheel.
"Lawd, *Jesus*," she whispered, "if the devil ain't got one more thing
on his mind."

She waited a minute.

"Try it now, Mama."

"Hol' on, Maddy." She pulled the tail of her dress above her
knees, pressing down on the gas pedal. The motor caught.

Daddy watched us from the side of Mr. Sandifer's office. He was
a whole man, regardless of his ties to Jesus, the drinking, and the
thinning hair on his chest. But his manhood had been buried,
paralyzed.

Mama put her arm over the edge of the seat and backed out of
the scrap yard. Daddy had lost the gas cap somewhere between the
pool hall and the back roads of the county. An oil rag had taken
its place; it flew high in the rearview mirror, stuffed into the hole

where the fumes took over the surrounding things: the pasture, the cow manure, the worm, the things that ate the worm.

"I hope this heat let up," said Mama as she pulled the bonnet from her head and shook the split ends out of it. "It's taking my hair out."

The Negroes worked in the field. They cut away at the weeds: most of them standing with a wishbone in their backs, turning their straw hats downward, away from the sun. A line of barbwire fenced them in for miles. They were melting.

"Why's everybody so scared o' Jesus?" I asked.

The cross dangled from the rearview mirror. Its still-clean surface formed a smooth bend around the edges. Mama held it firmly, whispering about the figs with her driving hand on the wheel.

"I don't think we really 'fraid o' Jesus," she said. "We just owe him something—the same way we pay the 'lectric company to keep the lights on."

"You don't know Jesus, Ma."

She snapped. "I do know Jesus!" she said. "It don't matter if he don't wear no robe or nothing. We owe him. And if he don't get what's owed him, your daddy be in his grave 'fore we can say amen."

The barbwire had run out, the Negroes long gone. And the bonnet in Mama's lap was curdled, still. The hairs of her head crawling again.

chapter
fourteen

I had that summer flu. All I could do was lie under the covers and trace the circles of dust on my wallpaper. I heard voices in the kitchen: Mama's and two other women. They opened their mouths to speak, the sounds of flesh rising.

"That boy with the loose head," said the first voice. "You know the one."

They sipped away at their coffee. One pausing to lead the conversation. Another to control it.

"Who?" asked Mama, her voice fading into a whisper.

They all whispered now.

"God as my witness," said the second voice, returning.

"When this happen?" asked Mama between the two.

The first voice sipped her coffee, the liquid still spiraling. "Early this morning," she said. "On Commitment."

Mama paused. "Lawd, have mercy," she said. "Ain't nothing out there but a headache. When the service?"

"I don't know, child," said the first voice. "You know they keep black folks out longer than they do whites."

"Ain't that the truth," said the second voice.

"Yeah," said Mama, "I heard they keep the bones too."

"What you say?" said the first voice.

Mama raised her voice now. "That's what I hear tell," she said. "They keep the bones for scarecrows."

The other voices laughed. "That's the fanciest thing we ever heard!"

"That's just what I hear tell," said Mama. "They use them bones to draw the crows out there."

"Where?" said the first voice.

"Out to the scrap yard and so on," said Mama.

"Now, I done heard a lot o' things," said the second voice. "But I ain't never heard of no white man saving a nigger's bones."

"What they do with the heart?" asked one of them.

"They give it to the dogs," said Mama.

"Who you telling," said the second voice.

"Anyhow," said the first voice, "they say that boy was coming from Commitment when Diamond hit 'im."

"That's what I hear tell too," said the second.

"Well," said Mama, "reckon Landy gone have to use the wood from the hog pen. It's already fixed for death."

"That boy was cursed from the get-go," said one of them. "Him and his folks dying the same way—machines."

"What his granddaddy gone do?" said Mama. "He so used to praying over everybody else."

"Ain't that the gospel," said the first voice. "Not one soul in Pyke County prayed up enough to bless the deacon."

They all sipped.

"It's all in the Lawd's will," said Mama.

With this, they pushed the chairs out from under them, talking about Commitment Road and the killing. One car pulled out and I finally saw Miss Roberta Christian walking across the road to her father's house, her hands in the air.

Willie was dead.

A week later, I walked down the aisle of Owsley Sanctified Church—a place I had not visited since my sin of putting a naked lady on the first page of Genesis. The walls were filled with a darkness that sloped into a fragile, open-ended backbone. That emptiness that God took no part in. They were all sinners, whispering about the boy with the loose head and how that white man's motor had knocked him clean through the air.

The pastor leaned over Mr. Rye, telling him about how he needed some carpet in the place. "The church folk ain't been paying their tithes," he said, running a wide finger across his face. "*Jesus getting mighty dark around the edges.*"

They said that Mr. Diamond left Willie on the side of the road. Willie had worked for him all his life, stocking the post office into some type of order. Mr. Diamond knew that Willie Patterson had a loose head and didn't know the difference between a Cadillac motor and a Ford. He thought they were all the same. His granddaddy had always taught him to ride his bike against the traffic so the cars could see him coming. He was paranoid about something happening to him.

Landy Collins looked tired, sitting there in the front row. He had been up all night fashioning the pine into a rectangle, carving the insides of the tree out and aborting it in the woods somewhere. I sat in the bench behind him, watching his head slowly lean backward from the deep sleep that overtook him.

The casket was closed, and I didn't see one flower. They say that when Mr. Diamond hit Willie, the blood darkened the earth.

Willie didn't see him because he had a loose head. The papers said it was an accident. Mr. Diamond was blinded by the fog and didn't see Willie on the bike. He didn't see that grown-ass nigger riding that bike with those Chuck Taylors because the fog was thick on Commitment Road.

The church windows on each side of the aisle gave air to a wide ray of light over *Jesus*. The choir began to talk about Willie: the casket would be not open but closed, because his grandfather couldn't take the gossip going into the ground with him.

Suddenly, I remembered my grandmother's words, words that had become buried underneath a stream of urine from a sick woman's bladder: "Never forget the man who teaches you how to open your mouth. You and him talk the same language. You are one. Nobody else will know him like you know him. You are two people from the same spirit. You are one." Everything had come to me: Miss Diamond shooing Willie away from the window that day after school because she did not want him to tell me. Because she knew that he had seen her husband, Mr. Diamond, pull back the hairs on Laurel Pillar's head and rape her; a woman always knows when her sheets are dirty. I wasn't waiting on the world to apologize to me. She was. And on those nights when Mr. Diamond kissed the cleanliness from her, after a night of talking about the Chevys and Fords, she knew that she had smelled the rape of a woman on his breath: the same way I had torn Hitler out of the history books because I knew how many Jews he'd killed. The world was inside of her now. It went down from Mr. Diamond's penis to her vagina. She was carrying around a rape inside of her. Her husband had been fed the milk of a rapist. Somewhere, racing on a wire of thoughts in Big Mama's head, she had trusted that God would protect the black baby in her arms, that although she had been fed the same milk, He would spare her the taste of the rapist—for she had already paid the price. But the other baby, the white one, she had forgotten to pray for, the spoiled milk traveling through the text of his stomach and absorbing him.

Yeah, Miss Diamond had felt that day coming, the day when she could no longer keep Willie from telling the truth, the moment her husband would run down a boy with a loose head and kill him. Because the doctors had not taken away Willie's common sense: what it was to hear a woman scream because a man's penis was shattering the glass in her throat.

The law found Willie's body on the wrong side of the road. It wasn't facing the traffic like his grandfather had taught him, and since no one saw what happened, they took Diamond's word: he had blamed it on the fog. Now Willie lay in a casket with the sun shining through the northern window of the church, marinating his body into the pine.

Landy had done a good job on Willie. There was room in there for Willie. He had paid attention to Willie. He knew that a man Willie's size never would have fit into a narrow box. He didn't use the boards of the hog pen. He went deep into the woods and closed his eyes to think about the shoulders, the large head, the arms, the fat around the waist, the unusual circumstances that would go into that box. Everything had been taken into account. The way Willie kept his head to the side all the time, the low self-esteem of a man who worked long through the night for a bag of potato chips and a soda, the way he combed his hair to the side when the sun was going down; everything Willie had ever been was inside that box.

The flu had left me. Mama stayed home to prepare the food. She knew that Willie was nothing but dead. She had rutabagas to sit, and there was nothing she could do about a nigger with a dead scorpion on his mind.

The pastor tapped Landy on the shoulder. He woke suddenly and apologized for falling asleep before service. He looked around, and when he saw me sitting there, he did nothing. He was a grown man. I was a child who saw too much in him. I could never have him. He looked at me that way. I had some growing up to do, long after being a witness to a sickness and passing history.

The choir stood for the opening prayer: the white *Jesus* hung over them. His hands were nailed to the cross, His blue eyes downward, viewing the hole in His side. The church was barren, only a few pictures of Jerusalem and some artificial flowers in the podium vase. They were all talking about my sin. I knew it. I felt the countless eyes at my back, thickening into a bowl of brown sugar that glazed my skin into a fine, well-treaded syrup. It was not about the church tithes and the maroon carpet the pastor needed to match the choir's robes. It was about the death of a bastard and a sinner's fire-engine-red lipstick. It was about a child sent to take care of a whore who couldn't get into hell if she tried.

"Lawd," said the pastor, "we're gathered here today to celebrate the life of Brother Willie Patterson." He took a handkerchief from his breast pocket and wiped his L-shaped sideburns. His three-piece suit was the color of homemade wine after the grapes had soured and turned burgundy. "I say 'celebrate' because it's the omega. We are to rejoice at a man's end and forgive the unjust. Listen to me now. I said we are to *forgive* the unjust." He wiped his mouth now, eyes closed. "Can I get an amen?" The church went *Amen*.

"Folks," he said, "it was so hard for the Lawd to forgive us that He had to send His Son. He couldn't do it all by Hisself." He opened his eyes to the sunlight now, pulling his trousers over the fat in his gut. "Can I get an amen?" The church went *Amen*. "How can you love the Lawd and hate your neighbor? You don't have a choice in forgiveness. No repentance. No God. Do you hear me talking to you now?" He spoke in tongues. The church hears him. They say they hear him. "Ain't no such thing as half. Half what? Half hell?" He laughed a little, pointing his finger to the floor. "'Cause lemme tell you something, folks. You walk 'round here filling your head with disease, I guarantee you hell is the only thing you gone get. All hell. Not no half hell. Ain't no such thing as that." The church went *Amen.* "Don't come up in Owsley acting a fool, now. I know the sinners. I know 'em all. I got they address. I got they first and last names. And if you ain't heard nothing about my Jesus, then let me tell you. I got Him right here." He picked up the Bible and traced the letters with his fingers, showing it to the choir, then to the crowd. "Guess what, church? I know where you're going. It ain't hard. Do you hear me talking to you now?" The church went *Amen.*

Landy Collins moved around with the edge of his ears flattening out. He had seen my breasts. He was glad that he had left me standing there. I was a young sinner. I had time to fuck up and pray about it, but he knew better. He knew that it was wrong to stretch out my hole so close to a sick house.

"Let us pray here for Brother Willie and his elder, the deacon," he said, holding out his hand to the crowd. At the same time, Miss Birch, the bus driver, walked in carrying a vase of lilies. "Come on up here and join me, Deacon."

The church folk turned around. Out came a fragile man, Willie's grandfather, the gray in his eyes bordered by cataracts. He held on to the arms of the benches, taking his slow time down the aisle; the suit cloth dragged him down as he reached midways of the small church. The front seat was cold, save the flesh of Landy Collins moving around to check the measurements of the box, to make sure Willie was comfortable enough in there.

"Let us pray," said the pastor, helping Willie's grandfather to the podium. "Lawd, give us the strength to overcome the evil over this place. I don't know much about Brother Willie here, but I can pray that heaven is the place for him. Heavenly Father, watch over the deacon this morning. He tired, Lawd. He need you, Lawd. I wouldn't have said it if I didn't know so myself. Help us, Heavenly Father. In your namesake, we pray. Amen."

The choir sang:

> *It's gonna rain.*
> *It's gonna rain.*

The pastor's wife hollered. She fell against a man who didn't know what to do with her. The ushers immediately ran to her side, fanning her and pulling her dress down. *Jesus* was there. Nobody but *Jesus* owned Mississippi. There wasn't enough dirt and holes in the graveyard to keep up with the bodies out there, the ghosts hanging from the trees, the sinners.

> *Lawd, you better get ready.*
> *'Cause it's gonna rain.*

Miss Birch didn't know what to do with herself. A sober woman with *Jesus* so apparently missing from her life. Her hands disturbed her. She couldn't train them. The devil was inside them, spreading the nerves of her sobriety through the vase of Willie's lilies.

> *God sho'll know the rainbow sign*
> *It won't be water, but fire next time.*

Pyke County, Mississippi. A place where the dead lived. The road so long and rugged that time became a blur. Cold things lived there. People with thin blood and love enough for survival. Nothing else.

The clouds moved ahead. We took the pine box out to the cemetery and lowered it into the ground. The only men who knew the truth were dead now, including Uncle Sugar. A man without a voice is a dead man. He opened my mouth and gave me the word. And I, in turn, gave it to *Jesus*.

chapter
fifteen

It was early morning. Mama stood near the mailbox talking to Mr. Diamond. His hands were behind his back, propped at the waistline. The truck's motor hummed behind him. Mama patted him on the shoulder as he looked out past her, out into the earth, nodding.

What would he have done had I asked him to open his mouth? Had I lain him on a metal table and stuck a tube into the opening in his esophagus and drained Big Mama's milk out of him? I wanted to dissect him. It was his body that I'd traced out of the encyclopedia. The modeled structure was shaped like him, the narrow figure, the ribs of his chest tunneling beneath the shoulders, the yellow arms bent at the elbows as if he had been holding an infant. His lips were perched. He could not loose the Negro breast from his mouth. After all these years, it was still there, covering the light in his face, flesh-heavy.

Mama asked something of him. And he turned around, lifting his shirt from the backside. He pointed toward his kidneys. Mama put her hands on his back and nodded. And before they separated, he reached out his hand to her. She patted it and began to walk back toward the house with her head down.

She was in the kitchen now, moving something around. And when I met her there, she slowly opened her mouth. "Diamond got a worm in his back," she said. "We gotta get to praying 'fore it split him up from the inside."

She picked up the mason jar that housed the lizard and opened the lid. The lizard began to climb the glass, its neck coming up from the surface. Mama put her finger on top of it. The unbalanced body, the pulse of its throat vibrated. She pushed it back down and closed the jar. "If your daddy come," she said, "tell him I went to pray for a kidney."

The sky was growing dark. I was sitting at the kitchen table when Daddy came home with a wad of money in his hands. The look in his eyes was a tip. The money wasn't good. It had tainted him.

"Where your mama?" he asked.

"She went to church," I said. "They're trying to find Diamond a donor."

"Why?" he asked, puzzled. "What's wrong with him?"

"He needs a kidney."

He laughed so high and so above himself that he almost fell on the floor. "That's what he gets," he said, holding his stomach. "He shoulda paid me my money."

"A man can't help what he needs," I said.

He paused.

"Where'd you get that money?" I asked.

He walked over to the window and looked out into the empty backyard. He stuffed the money in his pocket. Suddenly, he asked: "What size foot your mama got?"

"Nine."

"Okay," he said, taking a pick from his back pocket and picking his Afro. "I gotta run. Hattie Mae car quit on her up the road a piece."

He paced the floor a moment. He had been in the same space Mama had been, picking up the glass-trapped lizard. In his laughter, he shook the green, watching the tiny bones in the neck, the winding tail, triangular. "Look how small the neck is," he said. "If I squeezed my fingers just hard enough, I could paralyze it."

He then went into the backyard to search for the red gas can. I followed.

"What's wrong with you?" I asked.

He had this big, wide smile on his face, as if he had gotten over on Mr. Diamond and the rest of the white men.

"Tell me what's the matter with you," I said.

He looked up at me. "Ain't got time right now, Maddy," he said, laughing from his gut, setting his eyes on where the hog pen used to be. "Tell Pip I didn't mean nothing that day. Just checking on her."

"Where'd the money come from?" I asked.

He patted me on the head, the red gas can at his feet. "Nothing," he said. "Don't go worrying yourself over me none. Your mama need something decent on her feet."

He grabbed the red gas can. "I gotta go," he said. "Hattie Mae be waiting."

"You can't spend what you don't have," I said.

"Ah," he said, closing his eyes to the air, "but I do. I got hope now, and ain't no man in the world gone take it from me."

He stepped down off the back porch.

"Not this way," I said.

He kept walking, disappearing around the corner of the house.

Midnight had come. I lay down in the hallway, listening to Mama read from the Book. She'd pause and start up again, waiting for Daddy to walk through the door. She stopped reading and sighed heavily. The faucet leaked. She began counting the number of times the water hit the basin. One. A pause. Two. A short pause. And thereon until she became familiar with the pattern. This noise kept her company until she forced herself to start over from the beginning. One . . . Two . . .

The numbers embedded themselves in my memory. She was teaching me subconsciously, the way she'd taught Daddy. The rhythm opened my mouth. I began to count with her, stressing each vowel sound of the numbers.

A motor passed by on the open road. She stopped counting and opened the kitchen door. The rumbling moved farther away from the house. She didn't move. She stood there holding her stomach.

One . . . two . . . a long pause . . . What was she waiting on? Did she not remember the dark cavity of space between her legs that kept her in bed for a whole week? She said that she had gone to use the bathroom and her panties were stained in the middle part, a yellow cream leaking from her vagina. She said that her stomach was hurting; the bird's nest had become infected. She sat up in bed with a bottle of vinegar, pushing it up through her stomach. When Daddy came home, he denied ever giving her a disease. He said that she had caught something from the misses, something had crawled inside her as a punishment for not wearing underwear. She took his word but left the house in the middle of the night, holding her ribs until she reached Jackson, Mississippi.

Surely she had been there before, in the hospital with the machines, although she hated doctors. She had been there in a white room, metal stirrups holding her feet, as a man in a white coat was pulling the yellow cream out of her and placing it on a square piece of glass, looking at it under a microscope. She herself had been diagnosed that night. The morning after, she opened her purse to pull out a handkerchief and the pills of penicillin rattled under the force of her arm.

This is what happened when she prayed out loud. She did not know that she was not only talking to *Jesus,* but she was talking to me too. I knew that Mr. Sandifer's wife had, indeed, paid her for the work at her house. But that she'd spent the money: she paid Jesus up. And the yellow cream that had come from her vagina was the disease of a cowardly man, an inconsiderate man.

The moon shone through my bedroom window. It formed a straight line across the tips of my toes. It seemed that people in Pyke County ignored the fact that they could touch what they loved. I looked at it, the moonlit bar across my feet. What if the moon had been a physical thing? What would I have done with the moon in my hands? These thoughts, among others, captured me. I was a child who wanted to eat what I could not feel; things without normalcy, like Daddy's alcoholism, listless things like Aunt Pip's breast cancer, the moon.

A car pulled up in the yard, a calm machine of little noise. This time it was Jesus. Daddy said something in the darkness. And Jesus let him go. Before he entered the house, Mama rushed back to the couch and opened the Book.

Daddy walked through the door.

"Faye," he said, "I got something for you."

Her head was still in the Book. She spoke softly. "What is it?"

"Close your eyes," he said.

She seemed unsettled. "Jesus killed a man, Chevrolet," she said. "What you tryin' to do? Get yourself locked up in Missi'ppi State?"

He never told her what he'd learned at the penitentiary: Jesus had killed no one. But this was her fear. Somewhere deep down, she thought that Jesus would cut Daddy's throat at the vein and she'd find him hanging from a tree in the front yard: fear that she would become a widow like Fat or Miss Hattie Mae or that the world would somehow blame her, as the world had blamed Eve.

"Come on, baby," said Daddy. "Close your eyes."

As she did this, he placed a cardboard box on her lap. I lay on my stomach, watching him verify that her eyes were closed. "Okay," she said.

He pulled out a box cutter from his back pocket and gave it to her. "Here," he said.

She pushed the lever up on the side of the knife and cut the box open. It was a pair of new shoes. "Lawd, Jesus," she said, measuring them against her feet. "I can't wear some'n so fancy, Chevrolet. Got enough bunions already."

"How come?"

Mama shook nervously. "'Cause," she said.

"What's wrong witchu?" said Daddy. "You wanna wear hand-me-downs for the rest o' your life?"

"Quit that, now," she said. "Maddy hear you."

"She know!" he yelled. "The whole town know. Them boys on Factory think I ain't got no pride for myself."

He was drunk. "My wife on the Pyke County hill yes-maamin' and no-maamin' for the rich. That's why I can't get paid on time. The white folks think I'm free-willing!"

She looked down at the shoes. "I ain't got time for this, Chevrolet," she said. "I been out all day prayin' for a kidney."

Daddy took a seat beside her. "How you 'spect to do that?" he asked. "Ain't no doctor this side o' Mississippi gone put a nigger's piece inside o' Diamond." He laughed. "Which one o' you's puttin' out?"

"I couldn't tell you," said Mama. "We used numbers. You never know with numbers."

"Crazy," said Daddy, "every one of you. Taggin' yourselves like cattle."

Mama sat quietly for a moment, then whispered: "Where the money come from?"

He grew angry again. "You need some'n decent to walk around in," he said, pointing to her feet. "You's flat-footed. All your shoes got lead in 'em."

"Chevrolet," she whispered, "the money."

He stood over her and picked up the shoes: "*Jesus*."

Mama said nothing. He had said this name so many times that she couldn't tell the difference anymore. She picked up the Book and began reading again. Her silence hurt him. His face was disturbed with the pain he had caused her, a pain that not even liquor could have numbed. He tried to touch her. His touch shook her body, the impact going from her arms to her hips like a woman who bathed outside in the nude.

"Faye," he said as he dropped the shoes beside her and put his hand over her face.

She ignored him as she spoke out loud from the Book. He walked to the far end of the kitchen table and stared at her. Her voice echoed throughout the house. His drunkenness no longer disturbed her. After he realized this, he walked over to the faucet and silenced it.

chapter
sixteen

Mama's flesh was like stone. She was naked on the covers of her bed, her feet turned inward, her toes stiff and useless. The body that she had been so ashamed of was out in the open, spread across a row of doves flying up through the covers in rows of threes. Her legs were open; the scars on them from work took the shapes of giraffes, elephants, and four-leaf clovers that patterned themselves underneath her thin hairs. Her fat was solid now, not loose. Hard. The side of her thigh, her hip, was as if no human being had ever touched it. It was loveless, as thick as the dust of Mississippi. The nest of fur between her legs was tangled and sat straight up from her pelvis, dark. And when her breasts came down beside her, the nipples stood erect with a hint of pink the color of Pepto-Bismol. What mattered most to her, the looseness of her arms, was even, at this point, as straight as a piece of wood with no curves at all. She lay in bed with her eyes unbatted, her hands at her side, the palms open and without movement.

I went to touch her face. "Mama," I said, "what's wrong with you?"

She didn't say a word, just stared into a dark place. A tiny bird landed in the window. Even in its size, it carried the shape of

Mama's large body. The small feet that perched it into place, its ankles going up to its full belly where it seemed to have looked pregnant, the fragile neck.

A sheet of paper was pinned beneath her shoulder. I reached for it. "No," she said. The hand that she had once used to love me was tightly wrapped around my wrist, its grip hurting the bone.

"What is it?"

She let go of me and almost instantly went back to her position, lifting her chin only a little higher to land evenly on the pillow. "They took her milk," she said.

These words rested on her tongue so heavily that her mouth remained open, the odor of her life coming up through the cracks of her teeth. When the bird began to chirp, she rolled over on her side with her eyelids low.

"Who?" I asked.

She was so very distant. The sheet of paper lay beneath her, opened.

"Men," she said.

When her throat stressed these syllables, it forced a hollow breath of wind to toughen her lungs. The base of her neck, the dip there, was pulsating. The nerves in her body, the elephants, giraffes, and four-leaf clovers had been pushed from her legs, up from her abdomen to her throat. They were sitting there underneath a widespread tree, nesting on their roots, their hind legs, waiting for her to let them go.

"What are you saying, Mama?"

My questions seemed like broken thoughts of ignorance. Every time she widened the air in her mouth, her stomach rose. There was no glass in her throat, only stone. And when the bird flew away, she showed no emotion at all. It was as if a small thing had come and passed to confuse her with its noise.

"This is why, I tell you," she said, quickly lifting herself to grab me by the arm. "Sit down with time."

Everything came from men, the instinct of being a woman, because they had supposedly created me, doused me with their knowledge so much that I'd been walking around with their words, their acts of boredom, in the passage of time.

"I do."

She hurriedly let go of me, her crawling hair landing back against the pillows. Her hands remained curved as if she still had my bones in them.

"No," she said, "you too green." She straightened out her fingers and rested them on her stomach where she'd begun touching the rows of fat. "I wish I could keep you in glass. Just look at you and save you from the world."

"The misses came for you this morning," I said.

She gave little emotion, although her eyes opened and appeared curious. "What you tell her?" she asked.

"I told her you were sick," I said.

"Sick," she said. "You don't stop cleaning house 'cause you sick."

I wanted to tell her how the misses looked, her pink face relaxed to the nerves in her lips, how she seemed not to care because there was a Negro girl in the backseat holding her fingers upright. And the rustle of the tires in the driveway, slow and weak as its driver, shallow.

Daddy came walking through the front door. We had studied his routine, a stop near the kitchen window, a look out at the vanished hog pen. "Maddy," he said, "come go with me."

I smelled his work, the little hours he'd spent at the scrap yard with Mr. Sandifer, the oil in his clothes. He had not been drinking, only smoking a cigar between the hours. He walked down the

hall until he finally came to a complete stop in the doorway.
Mama's nude body was a burden to his eyes. "What the hell's wrong
witchu, woman?" he asked.

Mama did not change her position. "Go with your daddy," she
said to me. Her face was cold and stern.

"Yes, ma'am."

When Daddy saw that she was in her own world, not his, he
walked over to the bed and shook her. "You done went crazy?" he
said.

She didn't open her mouth, the contents of her voice kept still
by the sharpness of his language. Daddy shook her again, and when
she moved his hand away, he slapped her on the thigh. "Come on,
Maddy," he said. "Let's go to Jolie's."

The sun was coming out through the trees. Although Daddy
showed no signs of affection to Mama, I could see her condition
on his face, how it bothered him that she had lost herself like that:
the silence broke.

"Why are we going to Mr. Jolie's?" I asked.

He looked out past the houses. I had never been to this side of
Mississippi. There were Negroes in their yards, the children playing with an antique wheelbarrow. A toddler sat in the dust, near
the small limb of a tree. He was privately watching the others. A
woman was needling a quilt on the front porch. Her head was into
her work. Two boys were sitting inside the wheelbarrow now. As
it began to roll, the others pushed the two of them over the legs of
the toddler. The woman on the porch put the fabric aside and
dusted him off. The toddler's legs hung in the rearview mirror. He
pulled away from the woman and began to rub them. Long after
we passed, I could still hear the pain in his lungs.

"We got a hog to kill," said Daddy.

His voice was straightened out by the anger of these words. It was man versus nature. It wasn't enough that he'd killed our hog in Morgan City. He needed another killing to make sure the dirt was packed down on the enemy.

"Mama says that if you get blood on you, the ghost'll follow you home," I said.

"What ghost?"

"From the dead," I said.

He laughed as violently as he had breathed when the bones of the lizard's neck were in his hand. "You don't have to worry 'bout that," he said. "A hog ain't got no ghost."

A herd of cows ran toward the edge of a barbwire fence, back again to the earth behind them. He tamed his laughter, saying, "Besides, we take the eyes out."

"Why?"

"'Cause," he said, pushing his knees up to the bottom edge of the steering wheel to guide the truck, "we ain't got no use for the eyes. Just the meat." The hair on his head was as strict and tough as wool.

"But that's where the blood is," I said.

He looked out at the roof of Mr. Jolie's house, a place I had never been. "Don't listen to your mama," he said. "She lonely."

Daddy was a man who hid what he desired until it came out in a wind of Pyke County gossip. This was what made him a man, his ability to cover up his goings-on enough to try to protect Mama and me from it, except for the night he slept with Aunt Pip.

Soon Mr. Jolie's house was in plain view. Each board was perfectly placed. The rectangular pieces of wood slatted against the square windows, one on top of the other, climbing into a triangle at the mounted roof. The branches of a large oak tree rose above it, into the white sky behind it. When my eyes came down from the oak, I noticed Mr. Jolie's daughter in the window. She was a quiet girl who rode bus number forty-three. She was as Willie had been, missing a part of her body that made her handicapped to the world and the people in it. One of her eyes was fixed by *Jesus*. A white spot covered it. Mama said that a blind eye was a blessed eye. It meant that half of the world could hurt you. And the other part, the part you could see out of, you could imagine, dream.

"Now," said Daddy, "it ain't nothing to seein' a dead hog. The dead can't hurt you none. It's the livin' you got to worry about."

The men behind Mr. Jolie's house hung their arms over the hog pen. They had grabbed their hats so much that they were permanently bent in the middle. Like Daddy, they killed.

"Come on," said Daddy as the killers beckoned for us to join them.

After we'd made it to the hog pen, Daddy put his hand on my head and looked at the other men. "How's it going?" he asked them.

The killers spoke at one time, moving aside to let Daddy see the hog up close. One of them looked down at me. His teeth were straight, and when he opened his mouth, it wasn't hard to tell that his wisdoms were missing. A tall man whose strength showed in his arms. "This you, Chevrolet?" he asked.

Daddy turned away from the hog and smiled at me. "Yeah," he said, "that's me."

"It ain't hard to tell," the man said, pushing his thin sleeves up to the elbows. "What part of that hog you want?"

"The eyes," I said, looking into his mouth, the smoothness of his tongue against his throat.

"You can't do nothing with the eyes," he said. "They ain't got no meat in 'em."

The hog squealed. And when one of the other men moved away from Daddy, I saw it, the quiet eyes, the mouth hanging. It was as nude as Mama. The small feet, the way the gut hung over the pelvis, lost.

I looked up at the man with the wisdom teeth missing. He laughed and folded his arms as if he controlled my vocabulary. "What you gone do if you take them eyes home and they just get up and walk off?"

"Find out where they're going," I said.

All the men laughed. The other men laughed and held their bellies and grabbed their killing hats. The man with the missing wisdoms leaned toward me. "Well," he said, "hogs ain't got no nerves. So you ain't got that to worry about."

The hog started to whine, and the man with the missing wisdoms ran over to the pen. They began to measure the feet, the head. One of the other other men made a square with his hands. The others watched him, how the space between his fingers was too far apart for them to agree.

"Where Jolie?" asked Daddy to another one of the killers, who'd tagged his keys on to his pants. You could hear them against his thighbone, chiming in the same kept rhythm of a man whose patience was in the middle of his body.

"Inside," said the man with the keys.

Daddy turned his back to the pen. "Well," he said, "go get him."

The man with the keys looked at him strangely. "How much you paying?"

The other other men grew silent. They knew that Daddy's word didn't count. And when Daddy felt the tension around him, he looked up at the oak, the widespread limbs.

"I don't know," he said. "Me and Jolie got a understanding."

"You better," said the man with the keys. "Don't take nothing you can't pay for."

"Nigger," said Daddy, pulling out a row of dollar bills, "I got money."

At that time, Mr. Jolie walked out of the house. He was a quiet man but moved with a harshness about him. He was a man who'd built his own nest. For this reason, he was respected in Pyke County. When you saw a man like that walk upon the earth, you had no choice but to respect his actions, the calm manner in which he timed his movements, perfect, detailed movements.

"She ready," said the man with the keys. The other men stood around him, their blurry faces melting into the clouds.

"All right," said Mr. Jolie. He walked toward the John Deere.

One of the blurry men shoved Daddy in the side. "Ain't she pretty," he said.

"Yeah," said Daddy, "that's a fine lady."

The men watched Mr. Jolie. They envied him.

"By the time I saved up for some shit like that," said the man with the keys, "I'd be so old I couldn't even shift the bastard."

"But you could still climb on top of 'er," said one of the blurry men.

They all laughed. Mr. Jolie looked back at them, his back to the seat of the John Deere with his feet on the gears. When he approached the hog pen, the men walked over to meet him.

Mama was somewhere pulling the bed across the room, re-arranging it to suit Daddy. He had seen her in the light. She didn't want him to remember any part of her flesh. This was what she felt. A man who saw you naked, in a moment when you least expected it, would run away. It was as safe to move the furniture, to clear his mind of her nudity, as it was to drown out the voice of an unwanted bird.

"Aw, hush up!" said the man with the molars as the hog rammed its head into the gate.

The pen was so very small. They had built it to fit the body of the dead. The perfect measurements: a space of an inch or so bigger than the hog's width, the wood stacked up above the length of the bones in its neck, closed in, captured, and fed until the body grew into its own healthy death.

"Let's go," said one of the other other men.

And as calm and quiet and hardworking as Mr. Jolie was, he climbed into the pen with the hog, took out a knife that would've reached my kidney from a small distance, and slit the hog's throat. He slit and slit and slit until that hog stopped squealing and its head fell over the blade. The blood came running down from its body like that of the dead bird, primitive and loose.

"All right," said Daddy, "move out of the way so we can jack 'im up!"

The man with the keys signaled for me to move. The hog's body lay in the mud, its head separate from its neck, the eyes open, still.

I stepped back only to notice Mr. Jolie's daughter behind an orange curtain, the tails of her hair hanging behind her ears. She'd been watching the men, as I had. And when she saw the blood on her father's clothes, she disappeared.

One of the blurry men backed the tractor up to the body, while the man with the keys climbed up on the pen and hooked a pulley to the oak. The ropes of the pulley made a dark noise, as if it knew the importance of its use.

"I got it," said the man with the missing wisdoms.

One of the other men hitched the hog up to the tractor and dragged it out of the pen. The man with the keys tied the hog's feet with the rope. When finished, he tugged on the rope to make sure the pulley was stable. He stood there with Daddy and the others debating over the amount of intestines and cheese and ham and chitterlings and cracklings and bacon they could each get from the kill. Mr. Jolie said he'd take off for the help.

"Good," said the man with the keys.

They crowded the hog.

"Come here," said Daddy, reaching his arm out of the group to touch me. The other men stepped to the side. Daddy pointed to the hog's ass. "That's a good load of ham there," he said. "We can eat another year off that."

The kill had recovered him. He looked at the hog's eyes, the sadness in them, and smiled. It was more innocent than the first. The first hog had done a terrible thing. It deserved to be killed. But this hog had done nothing. It gave a man more pleasure to disrupt innocence. It gave him power.

"The eyes," I said to him, "they're movin'."

"Naw," said the man with the keys, "he ain't bothered."

One of the other men said, "And his brain the size of a pea."

It was like a murderer telling the man he killed why he killed him and how easy it was for him to get away with it. "You still want the eyes?" said the man with the missing wisdoms.

Daddy touched me on the spine. "No," he said.

I backed away from him and the others. The man with the keys climbed on top of the tractor and shifted until the rope on the pulley began to tighten. The hog's body slowly lifted, his feet bound. Before long, the hog was hung in midair, the blood dripping from the widespread oak onto the ground.

"Where your ol' lady?" Daddy asked Mr. Jolie.

"She at the in-laws," he said.

"You mind if Maddy wait inside till we get done here?" asked Daddy.

Mr. Jolie looked at me: "How ol' are you?"

"Fourteen," I said.

He looked up at the orange curtains. His daughter was standing there with her hair in her hands. "Come down now," he said, as if he were coaxing a cat down from a high branch.

"Go on, Maddy," said Daddy with his knuckles in my back.

"Yes, sir."

They walked back to the hog. I watched them as I trailed backward to the back door of the house. The man with the missing wisdoms lit a cigarette and walked away from the others. As soon as I opened the door, I saw Mr. Jolie's daughter sitting cross-legged in a wooden chair. Her blind eye just as white as a bar of lye soap.

She didn't say anything. Those long tails of hair hung over her ears. She didn't think I was my daddy's child. My skin was too bright and clear. She looked at me that way like she wanted to ask me who my daddy was and what the hell was I doing in her house. I didn't know what to do. I took a seat in front of her on a brown sofa covered with a hand-stitched quilt.

The house was beautiful. You never realize how dull your house is until you go visit somebody who took pride in theirs. Mr. Jolie and his wife took great pride in their house. Every certificate their daughter had ever won was nailed to the walls. Small things completed them. A picture of a man with scarred fingers holding a baby. Two candles on the mantel held by iron stars. Black life-size dolls at the head of the kitchen table. Big lips painted in a bright red. Pillows on the couch with the names of *Jesus*, Moses.

"What you looking at me for?" said Mr. Jolie's daughter. Her legs were still crossed, the patches on her knees elephant-dark.

"Nothing," I said.

"You looking at my eye," she said. Her voice was strong, as if she had been born before. Some old tree was missing its roots. They were inside her lungs.

"No, I'm not."

"Yeah," she said, "you looking at it."

"My daddy sent me in here to wait for him," I said. "I'm not looking at your eye."

She uncrossed her legs. Her panties had a red spot in them where the lips spread apart. "Oh," she said.

"How come you never talk on the bus?" I asked.

"You so stupid," she said with her elbows on her knees. "You think 'cause people don't talk, they lazy."

"No, I don't."

"Yeah, you do," she said. "Like people who don't say 'Mississippi' all the way."

The men outside laughed loudly.

"You ever save the eyes?" I asked.

"Where'm I gonna put them?" She knew what I was talking about. She moved like she had tried to save the eyes herself.

"I don't know," I said.

"You don't even know what you talking 'bout."

"What's it to you?" I asked.

"A lot, if you want me to tell you the truth," she said, sitting up like she was mechanical. "Miss Diamond pass you?"

"Yep."

"I wouldn't have," she said, falling back into the wooden chair in deep breaths. "You can't talk to grown folks like that."

Grown men were out behind her house killing a hog. That's what grown folks did. The men who called themselves men. They raised and fed a pig and changed its name to hog and killed it. "I can spell Mississippi backwards."

"What you telling me for?" she said. She stood up from the chair and walked into the kitchen. "You thirsty?" she yelled.

"No."

"I am," she said, before turning on the faucet and running up a row of stairs with her feet hitting hard on her father's work. When she came back down, she had a crystal glass in her hands. "This is my favorite glass. My grandma gave it to me before she died."

"How old is it?"

It took awhile before I realized that I had turned completely around on the sofa, staring at her white eye.

"Crystal don't age," she said with a deep frown. "You know that?"

Imagine being left something that never aged. Every time you picked it up and used it and looked at it, it'd be the same age. I wanted to hold that glass in my hands as I sat there with my back to the certificates and watched her gulp down most of the water. How beautiful it was to watch her eye through that glass that her grandma had given her. So very beautiful. "No," I said.

There was a small level of water left in the glass. She slowly poured it down the sink, running back up the stairs.

"Where are you going?" I yelled.

"I'm going to hell, Maddy Dangerfield," she said, laughing loudly. "I'm going to hell!"

She never came back down the stairs. And I sat there looking out the window of her house, watching the hog, gutted now. Justice Bates had been killed like this: the rope pulled tightly around the bones in his neck, the position of his face on the pulley, his arms tied around his back, the Mississippi branches forming a vein behind him.

chapter
seventeen

Mama was at the side of the house hoeing up a new row for the garden. A white scarf was tied around her head, covering her crawling hair. She was a long-winded woman when it came to her work. Anything less was senseless. The signs of Deuteronomy were there, changing her, shaping her into an obedient wife. She had come to terms with her illiterate husband, the choice she had made when she was too young to know the difference. And that her tongue was a muscle of its own actions. She had taught Daddy the vocabulary of the liquor labels. But in the meantime, she had chosen to neglect that while she was teaching him the language, she was accepting his alphabetical solitude: she had given him the ceremony of alcoholism; he was no longer married to her but to his handicap. She had become his mother, showing him the colors of stop signs and grocery-store commodities to help him cheat himself out of belonging to a literate world.

She had pulled up a full row of earth. By now she was walking behind her work and spreading the seeds of tomatoes from a brown paper bag. She had moved the furniture in her bedroom again. This is what she did when the pain got to her: she moved things.

The hoe began to dig into the ground again. She kneeled beside the second row's beginning and smiled. She measured its width alongside the first with her foot and went back into the ground, the iron hoe swinging blades of glass. Just over her head was a singing sparrow. Its body was like hers, like the bird in the window the morning of her speechlessness. The flat feet hooked on a bracket of thin lumber, the wide mobility of the stomach. For a brief moment, she looked up at it, one hand on her hip, as she began to hum:

> *His eye is on the sparrow*
> *And I know He watches me.*

The hoe went back into the ground. Daddy was coming around the corner of the house with the red gas can. He shook it and looked into the rubber nozzle for any traces of gasoline. When the effect displeased him, he sat the can alongside the second row and paused.

Mama went into her bosom and pulled out a set of folded dollar bills. She straightened them out and counted each one with a wet thumb. Daddy pointed toward Factory. His hair was tinted with a touch of mahogany where the sun had begun to singe it. "Give it here!" he yelled, as if Mama had aggravated him.

He was already disgusted by the empty jar above the stove. It was the first sign of her distrust in him. Her faith in God was growing, and he could sense that the moment would come when she would no longer keep her money in jars, her bosom, or anywhere else, because God would show her the destruction of a gambling man. Daddy snatched the dollar bills out of her hand and put them in his back pocket.

He picked up the gas can and trampled off.

"Don't spend it all," yelled Mama. "You hear me?"

She started to hum again, looking up for the potbellied sparrow in the trees. It was gone. But nonetheless, the glass vase in her throat tingled on the waves of heat around her. The feeling of someone staring at her caused her to look directly into the window. She stopped hoeing and closed her mouth. Her eyes were opened wide, the sun's glare burning them. She was beginning to feel something.

With a silent motion, she looked toward the kitchen window and called me to her.

Everything came into view: the perfect matted lime-colored prints left by the wooden boards of the hog pen, the heap of ants crawling in the dirt behind her with Daddy's footprint still in it, the limb where the bird had flown away and left it trembling.

Mama lowered her jaw, as if to let the air of the earth into her mouth. She put weight on the hoe. She was vast, her hips spread flat, the pelvis hidden. She handed me the brown paper bag and began to hoe again. Where she pulled up the earth, I planted the seeds. Now I was in her footsteps again. The bones that formed sentences, words that were invisible, paralyzing.

Grandma was near. And I thought about the morning of her death: the green shoes dangling from Mama's hand, how she did not call for the coroner until many hours later, after rigor mortis had set in to Grandma's body; her telling me how she laid upon Grandma's chest where the sick milk of her breasts made her cold, bare.

Mama was putting the hoe on the ground now. She sat down beside it and called me to her: "Come here," she said.

She touched the flesh of her stomach and spread her legs out. I put my head in her lap. For a moment, neither one of us spoke. But her mouth was opened to the heat of the sun, and the fumes from her body were beginning to rise.

She opened my mouth with her fingers.

Her hands were carved by mankind. All of her life she had been cleaning white folks' houses, burping their babies, and folding down the covers of their lives. Her life was not important. This, she believed, as the surface of her fingertips grew more and more rigid, coated with the work of duty on them. From time to time, she hid them from me yet believed that a woman's hands were her glory. I had found myself, several times, watching her large body lying still on the pillows of her bedroom, her lips like large caterpillars moving across her shadow in a wall of moonlight, her nose flat, her nose wide. These hands I most wanted to touch, to open the map of her duty in them. I wanted to eat the juniper from them, suck it out from the bone. But when I came close, the instinct of being a woman set in, and she woke up to find me standing over her, as she had her own mother, with my mouth at her fingertips.

Now she was pulling my face to her nose, smelling my breath. Then she relaxed my head again. The sparrow was singing on another branch, another world. "You don't have my milk in your mouth," she said.

She was high up, herself, up on a branch or a burden. She looked at the garden, her face coming down, away from my eyes. "When you was in my stomach, my titties swole up," she said. "You was so tiny, so tiny and . . ."

There was no egg in her throat now.

". . . I thought my titties would smother you."

She put her fingers back inside my mouth. "'Cause we all got milk, you see," she said, "but it don't come out the same way."

Her finger was on the muscle now, the tongue, pinning it down. My mouth began to fill with saliva. I swallowed it.

"I need to be close to her now," she said. And when she took her fingers out of my mouth, she closed her eyes and smelled them, taking the air in her lungs.

The clouds were opening up. Somewhere in heaven, Willie's own mother was putting her fingers in his mouth and sliding her nipple inside him. Because all things end where they begin.

chapter
eighteen

It had been a long day in Pyke County, where the darkest of black folks rose their hands to the clouds and swore they saw *Jesus* standing on the edge of the pastor's collarbone. He stood there fumbling through the pages of Deuteronomy and planting the words in a more solid, physical step forward, beckoning the church folk to come to him, saying: "And he humbled thee, and suffered thee to hunger, and fed thee with manna, which thou knewest not, neither did thy fathers know; that he might make thee know that man doth not live by bread only, but by every word that proceedeth out of the mouth of the Lord doth man live." He pulled a white handkerchief from his coat pocket and wiped his forehead. "Let the church say amen," he said. The church said *Amen.* "His word is the only true word," he said, looking down into the Book for help. "God is not only the truth. He is the answer." I looked up at him, watching the verse fold over in Mama's lap where she had touched the pages so many times.

We sat on the last row. It seemed like Mama prayed more now than ever. She prayed for everybody: the dead, the living, God and His bad headache that the world gave Him. She kept her eyes on Daddy. It had been a long time since he came to church. He was dressed in a black suit that was too small for him. The church folk kept turning around in their seats, whispering to one another, as the usher passed the offering tray to the row in front of us. She knew we didn't have the money. We had given it all to Jesus.

Daddy lowered his head. I sat between him and Mama—sometimes leaning my head on his nub and feeling the heat from it on my temples. He hung out at the pool hall so many nights that the cigarettes and liquor were in his clothes. A large fan centered at the back of the church blew all his sins into the small room. The church folk whispered.

"We will now read from First Corinthians, chapter ten," said the pastor, signaling for the ushers to count the money and post it on the Sunday-school blackboard. "There are, it may be, so many kinds of voices in the world, and none of them is without signification." He loosened his tie, wiping his forehead again with the white handkerchief. The church said *Amen*. His suit was shiny, a whale blue that seemed stitched too tightly at the hem. "Y'all don't hear me today." He walked away from the pulpit and threw his long arms toward the aisle, away from the microphone. "I said, y'all don't hear me." Willie's grandfather put one hand in the air. "Yes, Lawd," he said. He stayed neat. An old, neat man who had already taken my place. He had seen the dead, touched it, smelled it, let it go. A grandfather who dealt with Willie's death suddenly. The only thing he ever had to remember was the sound of a white man's motor, playing like a guitar in his mind.

"We must all come to Thee," said the pastor. "All the sinners, those living in hell as we speak." He raised those eyes to the walls of the church and pointed to the Apostles that were drawn by the Sunday-school children. "Look there, people. Now, you tell me that He can't live unless we want Him to." The church said *Amen*. "I don't know how much you love Him. But I love Him today." A lady said: "Tell 'em, pastor. Preach on now." He stepped backward and pulled on that whale-blue suit like it was all he had. "You can go to any other country in the world and see the king buried there. He just as dead as he can be, just laying there in a man's body. But the Lawd. Everybody looked. Everybody searched for His spirit in the Land, and nobody, not one Man, can tell you they saw His face." He shook his head. "Are you listening to me?" That same lady responded saying, "After while." "If you go to the Place, you won't find Him. Lemme tell you something church. If we could find Him, we wouldn't need Him."

The sweat from Daddy's nub dripped onto the bench, wetting the fabric in his pants. He grew nervous, widening his fingers along the thread of his clothes. His bare skin, across his knuckles with nothing but calluses and dark brown circles on them. Mama stared at him. She wore those shoes she loved. They were low-heeled, the bottoms rough and peeling. Those same shoes that Grandma squeezed lemons in before she became too old to walk in them. We sat there on the bench, just us three, listening to the whispers and the sound of that huge fan ticking in the back of the aisle.

A lady stood up and shouted. Her back was arched like those bones in the encyclopedia. I didn't recall the spelling of that part either. It was different from the bone in Aunt Pip's body. The lady took to her bones. She added a type of blackness to it, African blackness that moved like a white man had never put his hands on it. Those withering hands in the air, bitter and frail across the church walls. The ushers came to her side. "It's all right, sister," said one of them, fanning the lady's backside.

"Yes, Lawd," said the lady. Her eyes rolled in the back of her head. She put her weight in their arms and, with the mark of her shoulders, fell back toward the bench. She collapsed. The ushers looked around for the pastor.

"Give yourself up to the Lawd," he said. "When your way get muddy, you can't see no farther than the clouds, call on Him."

He picked up the Book and ran with it, picking up one knee between each step and calling on God. "I'm tired now." The bags under his eyes sweated down into his skin. "I say I'm tired now." A man took out a magnifying lens and turned around in his seat as if something were aching him. "We hear you, pastor," he said. "Preach to me."

Mama shook that leg back and forth against the wooden bench. She just couldn't keep still. The hairpins in her Goodwill hat were coming loose. She retightened them inside her crawling hair and pushed the alabaster hat down over her eyes. She tried her best to hide the tears. But I saw them. Daddy saw them. What he lost at the pool hall was one day's work for Mama. The more she put in the jar, the more she paid to Jesus, the more she took out for him. I realized that I had seen it with my own two eyes, Grandma going out to that hog pen slinging his arm over the gate. The blood from his body there on the floor and the funk throughout the house that I still smelled sometimes, because it had been so thick.

The pastor wiped his eyes: "Most of us live our lives on the ground when a 'mustard seed of faith' can relieve you of all things holding you down."

A thin line of chills ran up Mama's arm. That knee stopped shaking as she turned to look at Daddy sitting on the other side of me. The years were long between the two of them. She needed him to give up his long nights at the pool hall, stop drinking so much and straighten up his life. She didn't want to work for the white folks anymore. Always said she had to play the fool with them white folks, saying "yes, sir" and "no, sir" to them like she didn't have her own house to run. Those long days at the Sandifers' wore her down. Her back ached at night sometimes, when Daddy was down at the pool hall running up his bill with Jesus. She hated working for those white folks, but a married woman, with very little education. Simply put—a maid.

"Ann," Daddy said, stretching his hand across mine and finding it hard to grab hold of hers. She turned to look out the window.

"I know," she whispered.

The pastor stepped down from the pulpit with the Book in his hands. "If there be any testimony set forth by the children of God, let it be said at this hour."

No one said a word. The ushers walked up and down the aisle, pointing to the mothers of crying children, motioning for them to keep them quiet while the pastor was standing. "Now's the time to get that heavy burden off the line," he said. "Speak. The Lawd hear every word."

"Once," said Mama, looking clear through the church windows, her eyes wandering skyward, "I told my mama that I cleaned the fat between my eyes." The church folk turned around and looked around for the woman's voice. They mumbled. "I didn't have nothin' to give any man 'cause I came out with this fat between my eyes. If I frown too much, seem like it gone crawl clean off my face." Mama sat there with Daddy's hand in her lap, rocking herself back 'n' forth on the wooden bench. "But Mama. She say don't worry 'bout that none, 'cause that part be my birthmark."

The church folk whispered loudly. The pastor put his hands in the air. "Let her be," he said. "Go 'head, sister."

Daddy looked at her as if he wanted to quiet her down. His hand pulled tighter around her fingers. She embarrassed him by talking like that. It was embarrassing enough with him just sitting there with folks who knew more about what was going on in his house than he did. He wasn't a man with her sitting there telling them church folks all his business. But he knew that the townspeople

were never too mean to Mama. They wanted to be, but she was
such a hardworking woman that her fingers gained her the respect
she deserved, even if the respect was cruel.

"Lawd knows," she said, pulling that Goodwill hat down from
her crawling hair, "I got sinners in my house. I know every house
got sinners. But for some reason or else, the umbrella is over mine.
It stay dark there." She grew still for a moment.

The pastor walked down the aisle. "Tell it, sister," he said. "You
in the Lawd's house now. Tell it."

"Oh yes," she whispered. "It's always raining in my house. It rain,
I cry. It rain harder, I cry some more. I cry so much my birthmark
wearing thin now. It be shining like a river shine when the children ain't there no more. It just shine." She smiled, looking away
from the whispers with her still eyes. "I wonder why I work so hard
'n' don't see one penny of my money. Why sometimes it seem like
the devil got his arms so tight around my neck that I can't breathe.
He just take me. He whip me all the time. He just have his way
with me."

"Testify," said the pastor, unfastening the buttons on his whale-
blue suit.

"Pip ailin', yawl. She ailin' and I ain't done nothing for her.
What He gone do with me now? I ain't done nothing. She ailin'
and I ain't passed a glass of water through her kidney."

Although Mama had not told me, I knew that Aunt Pip was
dying—the cancer had spread to her other breast, echoed. I remembered those nights when Aunt Pip was asleep, the nights when
I could feel the lump move under her flesh: like the eyes of a dead
bird, a dead hog with the weight of its head coming down over a
sharp blade. I felt her now. And I knew that there was nothing
the doctors would be able to do to crush the spoiled milk inside of
her breast, her bones.

"Amen!" shouted a voice.

The pastor walked behind our bench and waved his hands over our heads. Daddy sat there with his chin down, afraid to look up at the many faces staring at him. He had gambled so much with Jesus that he didn't know what to do. The guilt was worse now. He sat there, clinging on to that black suit, his sins forming a cobweb around him.

"All I know is that He ain't done with me yet," said Mama. "Keep praying for me. Lawd knows, He ain't done."

The pastor touched her on the forehead, and she slid down under the wooden bench in front of us, on the floor like God had touched her. She screamed and yelled and the pastor kept his hands on her, crawling over the seat with his patent-leather shoes screeching on the panel. I moved over. Tears welled. That was my mama there hollering with her white panties falling to the crack of her ass. The ushers, with their white gloves, came rushing to her side. Strange black faces that I never would have trusted had I been on the outside. I pushed them away. Their hands smelled of olive oil as they touched Mama's backside, reaching out to feel the sweat on her.

"Let God," said a man. I heard him say it again and again, telling the crowd to get out of his way.

It was Willie's grandfather. Daddy got up from the bench, guiding his face from the crowd with his arm. They watched him walk down the aisle. Daddy had a rough life, but he had chosen that life. Mama had chosen her life too. But it was his Jesus that she had praised, not her own. And now she was reclaiming the one, the only, *Jesus*.

"Let us pray," said Willie's grandfather. We bowed our heads. "We come to you, Lawd *Jesus*. Me and the pastor here and the church. Take it from her, dear Lawd. I gave you my grandboy. You didn't steal him from me. It was his time. And I ain't had a better night's sleep in all my days. Pass that omega, dear Lawd *Jesus*. If I have any strength in me, give it to her. She need it, Lawd. Pass it to her, dear Father. You say not to stand under no shadow unlessing it's a tree—something made by You. Under no shadow of man shall one soul stand."

He put his hand on my forehead and spoke in tongues. His palm was sweaty. One of the ushers passed him a capful of olive oil. He pulled a handkerchief from his pocket and dowsed it with the oil before putting it on my forehead. Their voices seemed distant to me now. These strange black haunting voices that kept at me, lowering, raising my head with their rough fingers witnessing to me. "Rebuke him!" said the usher. They came down on me, grabbing my arms and speaking in those tongues that only God knew. I didn't know what I was supposed to feel or if that was what Aunt Pip felt when nobody understood—those doctors in Jackson touching her, the night she whispered Jesus' name on the front porch, the lizard crawling across her windowsill. Or what it felt like for Mama, who was trying to change her life and get her spirit right with God. I wondered what it was like to send me inside Aunt Pip's house and not be able to go herself, to stitch a pouch for the lizard so he wouldn't sneak outside the yard without her, what it was like being a woman who felt she made the wrong decisions, a lonely, miserable black woman scrolling through the pages of Deuteronomy.

I felt a familiar hand on me: "Come," said Daddy. He pried their praying hands off me and beckoned me to come with him. Mama pressed down on my legs with her hands. She meant it. I needed my *Jesus*. A man had cost her that, and it was all right if she lost it; but she would go to hell and back to make sure I had mine. There was no anger in Daddy's eyes as he stepped away from the witnesses and disappeared into the crowd.

The following morning, Daddy was sitting on the edge of his bed, naked. His silence had taken the place of Mama's. He picked up the Bible at the foot of the bed and put it down again. If only he had known how to read. If only he had paid attention to a different vocabulary, one outside of the bottles. He stood up, his penis hanging from his midsection, and closed the door.

Now he would not have to ask Mama what was wrong with her when she chose to lie nude on the pillows. Like her, it did not matter that he was missing something. He needed time to be alone with himself. How had it felt to be violated? What did women feel like when his hand went up their stomachs? Why couldn't he hold a fragile thing inside his hand without wanting to paralyze it? He was asking himself these questions, I was sure of it, the words of Deuteronomy staring back at him.

chapter
nineteen

I woke up from the nightmare. I dreamt that I lay in a bed of feathers. In the tiniest distance, I saw a floating vagina. It belonged to a woman with no face. She coughed and the hole opened up. I put my fingers inside. Somewhere in my thoughts, in the most peculiar manner, I thought of Daddy and the women, how somehow I'd carried the desire to push my fingers inside a woman's stomach. But I was not as he was. My desire was not of lust but of eagerness to see the power of a woman's abdominal muscles. As the vagina opened, I put my head inside. There was a baby inside a line of soft flesh; her thumb was inside her mouth. Her eyes were closed, feet crossed one over the other. I touched her. Her eyes came open. The movement of her pupils was slow, kind. I touched her again. Upon impulse, her thumb slipped out of her mouth. We were floating in water. Suddenly, I was part of a violent whirlwind and became detached from her. I reached for the cord and pulled it. She and I looked up, realizing that it was the force of the mother's cough that had separated us in the beginning. As I pulled the cord, she began to float toward me. She smiled at me as she grew closer. I was naked and cradling her head in a manner that required no human policy, only instinct. She sucked my nipple. It tickled at first. I wanted to believe that it hurt, but I couldn't bring myself to commit to it. And when she was full, she fell asleep in my arms. Her mother coughed again, and the force of it unbalanced me. She had pushed me out of the hole with her stomach muscles. I landed on the feathers, wet and cold, watching the sleeping baby go back up the hole, her dark face traveling through the distance.

I looked down at myself. A long tube was stretched across the feathers. As I felt the pulling of my own body, I noticed three babies hooked to my umbilical cord, their boneless feet going over the tip of the bed. I tried to pull it, but they were too heavy. They went over the edge of the bed, all three of them.

My hair was wet. I had drowned in the nightmare. And that drowning had taken my energy. I lay in bed, waiting for the use of my limbs to come back again. I could not move or open my eyes. Something held me down. The thought of moving was greater than anything that I had ever imagined. But I could not carry that movement out.

I thought of Big Mama in the cornfield, what it must've been like for some man to hold her down, rape her. The vision came in and out of my head at times. The vision of her screaming loudly, the birds flying northward over her, the white man's face turning red now, his eyes rolled back in his skull, Big Mama no longer screaming but lifeless. I pictured her sharp, angular voice. Raped. Her vagina being stretched apart from the outside in. The noise of strangers crossing an open road, those who could have neither stopped nor killed the rapist.

As I lay still, not only had Big Mama consumed my thoughts, but Laurel Pillar too. Whether her body was taken or given, abused or absorbed, so much had depended on a woman's hair. Every part of her beauty categorized by the length and history of it. It was then that I was glorified by the feeling of Aunt Pip losing hers. It hadn't mattered at all that it would no longer be a part of her. It was a beautyless thing. She had not gotten rid of her beauty. She had gotten rid of her rape.

I felt a hand over my breasts.

Then my eyes opened. And standing over me was Mama, her swollen hands going down over my breasts, checking me for signs of cancer. The muscles in her throat were rising now, like an un-digested egg in the belly of a snake, going up through a tunnel of blood and milk, surrounded by electricity.

The gossip traveled throughout Pyke County. The doctors had found a donor for Mr. Diamond. The number that Mama and the others had used at church had worked. Mama was in the yard talk-ing to Landy Collins. She pointed up toward the sky with one hand on her gut. And pulled out an envelope from her breasts, offering it to him. But he wouldn't take it. He opened the door of his truck and took out a sheet of paper, jotting down her vocabulary with a pen from his pocket. When done, he got back in his truck and disappeared through the trees, his engine in full-blown speed.

Mama returned to the house. She paused somewhere in the kitchen, quietly thinking of something that had troubled her: possibly the night she had been in her bedroom with one foot on the corner of her bed, the other solidly on the floor, lifting the fat of her vagina, pushing her fingers far up inside her, as she had done the plastic bottles of vinegar beside the toilet, looking for a relapse of yellow cream. Or the many nights she'd slept beside Daddy, counting the loaves of fat on her stomach, hoping that perhaps she could loose them. Perhaps it was neither. Only the silence that had begun to rise in her own body, because to forgive was much greater than anything she'd ever known, even in the testimony of God's house.

She made her way to my bedroom, her face in the mirror. The oval egg in her throat had grown larger over the course of a day.

"What's wrong?" I asked.

"Pip back," she said. "She broke the treatment."

"Did it work at all?"

"I don't reckon," she said, walking back toward the door. "Going to the misses. When I come home, be ready to go."

Her footsteps were melodic, programmed, like the dripping water from the faucet. It seemed that she was still counting the number of thumps in her head. This was the safest way, focusing on one object to memorize its rhythm. She walked this way until she reached the front door.

The misses was waiting for her. Over her shoulder appeared the toddler, sitting up in the backseat. He rubbed his eyes, his yellow hair almost white. He was still weak with sleep when Mama opened the door. He immediately reached for Mama, and her loose arm drifted from her lap, pulling him over the divided seat by one arm.

The sky was still white when she made it home again. Mr. Rye was in his yard with his hands behind him. It seemed that he was crumbling. We were all, in some way, falling apart.

Daddy was standing on the side of the house with the red gas can in his hand. He was far away from the vocabulary of the liquor labels, sober. The sun began to show on his face. He stared up at it with the likes of a prisoner coming out for the light that he so missed while in the company of his own solitude. He resembled the oval picture of Uncle Sugar, the side of his face molded into the age of a habitual mannerism, the neck up and tactful, the jaw-bone in a state of poised effort: something inside of him hung over the edge of his lips, as if he wanted to speak but could not find the words.

Mama looked at him and sighed. "We leaving now," she whispered, as if it no longer mattered that he was not listening.

Her hand was gripped tightly around the steering wheel. A narrow line of ink fell between the space of her index finger and thumb, disappearing behind the sleeve of her arm. It was not an act of child's play. The yellow-haired toddler of the misses had been sitting in her lap, drawing the thing in his mind on her skin.

We pulled out onto the road. A car approached us. The driver's head was octagonal, red like a four-way stop sign. His arm went up to it and combed back the hairs with his fingers. The figure beside him was motionless, the hair coming down over the shoulders, the face hidden along the sentiments of a dead bird, plump and straight.

A lump formed in Mama's throat. It was Mr. Clyde and his wife. There would be moments when he would take her out for a drive, away from the cold house in the woods, the cold memories. Mama looked over at me and smiled the smile of a cautiously trained woman: "Only the Lawd knows," said Mama.

Both the Pillars and Mama were driving at a slow speed.

Mama looked out ahead of her. The Pillars were closer, and the octagonal head of Mr. Clyde grew into focus, his eyebrows thick and wild. His wife's lips were immobile, straight like the line of ink between Mama's fingers. She sat next to Mr. Clyde, her face showing no form of expression, as if the reaction of her daughter's rape had permanently hardened her facial muscles to sadness.

Mama and the Pillars were face-to-face now. The wife did not budge or change her posture. Mr. Clyde stared deeply into Mama's eyes, as if he hated that he had ever given her anything on credit. I turned around and looked at them. He had run off the road. His wife stepped out of the car and walked over to the grass with her hands out, sitting on her knees with her arms facing the row of trees. Mr. Clyde sat in the car. It did not matter that he had worked my father in the field. He was burdened, his octagonal head banging against the steering wheel, his crying uncontrollable.

Mama looked at the line traveling up her arm, as if she had swallowed their hatred of her. "It took that oldest chap the longest time to get used to my nerves," she said, smiling. "He was like a Clydesdale at first. Them Clydesdales won't let you ride 'em till your nerves straighten out. They know fear."

A long piece of yellow hair had found itself rising on Mama's forehead. At some point, I imagined, the toddler had lain his pale head on her face. And without feeling it, the hair had become detached from his scalp. He was an active child, playful. The evidence of his character left on Mama's skin, limp and blond.

"When I die," she whispered, "don't cry over me none. I'll be in the Kingdom, and God don't need no help."

I wanted to tell her that I was afraid, that something was crawling on the back of my throat, a spider perhaps, wrapping its arms around my vocal cords, strangling my vocabulary the more we approached Commitment Road. Her voice began to fade in my ears. Her mouth and hands moved, but I heard nothing.

My thoughts were ahead of me. In no time, we were approaching Aunt Pip's house. The house appeared dark like when a child closes himself up in a closet to hide away from the world without knowing that the world stands behind him, trapping him.

Mama pulled up in Aunt Pip's yard. And before I stepped out of the car, I removed the yellow strand of hair from her forehead.

I opened the door to Aunt Pip's house. Her hands were out to me, her voice hoarse, crumbling.

chapter
twenty

A piece of glitter was glued to the inside of my hand. It glistened in the sun under the magnolia tree. Bare now. I picked at it with a silver teaspoon that I had carried from the house to catch the morning raindrops. The earth was beginning to light up again, the branches of the magnolia showering from above.

Aunt Pip was in the window, the green curtain pinned to the sides of the paneling. She played with her fingers, flexing the joints until her knuckles formed a row of mountains. We no longer needed to talk to use our voices. She was becoming forgetful, waking up in the middle of the night to touch her coarse hair, her hands frozen in the darkness because the machines had changed her body.

She reached for the area above her collarbone. Her hand was outstretched, moving alongside the space there. Her mannerisms were slow until she disappeared from the window altogether.

Fat had abandoned the oak tree. She appeared through the trees, her arms swinging beside her. Then she stopped alongside the road to dig out a patch of red dirt. When the amount pleased her, she tilted her head back and swallowed a large mass of it and threw the rest back on the ground.

I sat on the front porch next to the lantern, its clear symmetry holding still through the morning weather. But nothing, not even this lantern, would keep me safe now. To have held such an important device in my hands, an invention of light, was unsuitable, for I lived in the days of darkness.

"Where Pip?" asked Fat.

Blowflies had found themselves feasting on a piece of cantaloupe rind that I had thrown into the yard. Their wings fluttered about, as if they had discovered the sweetness of cantaloupe for the first time. How full of life they were, activated by a string of music in their collective buzzing.

I looked at Fat, the part centered in her scalp, the manner in which she stood on her bare feet. And wondered if a man had ever tried to take her down, attack her, with the courage it took to wrestle Laurel Pillar to the ground. "Asleep by now," I said.

She took a seat next to me on the steps. "How long she been out?" she asked.

"Not long."

We both watched the blowflies perch on the pointed edge of the battered cantaloupe. "Then I won't wake her," she said.

Her hands were swollen. She pulled her dress up to her thighs and let out a deep sigh. "Pip's bowels moved since you been here?" she asked.

"A little," I said.

She reached into her bra and pulled out a row of laxatives. "She must be stopped up again."

"I don't think she knows who I am anymore."

The corners of her mouth were red from the dirt. The blowflies bothered her, their constant buzzing echoing in the private area that contained them. She picked up her leg and stomped her heel on the ground. They flew away.

"It won't last long," she said. "She come in and out of it." She hid her face when she said this, adding: "Jesus got burnt out last night."

"I know," I said, although I had heard this for the first time.

"It don't matter none, though," she said. "He had insurance."

Fat looked down at her index finger. It had been split open, jagged, the cut going into her flesh diamondlike.

"What happened to you?" I asked.

She showed me the before and after of her hands, using one to create what the other used to look like. "A mad dog kept me up all night," she said. "I went for her and she bit me. That haffa got me good too."

With this, she got up and walked over to the magnolia tree. The petals had fallen to the ground. She picked them up and began to laugh. She was not the same Fat anymore. Something inside of her was changing. Now her head was low and forced to the bite in her hand. To have looked at her this way was to discover how unsafe she was in the world.

She returned to the steps of the house, seemingly more aggravated that the blowflies had found their way back again than at the fact that a mad dog had split her finger open. "Listen at it," she said, the howling of the animal now penetrating the earth. "If I ever see her again, I'm going to kill her."

"She didn't mean to," I said.

My words were useless to her. "Anger ain't never been no accident!" she said.

An emergence of sweat appeared on the tip of her nose. She was thinking about what she was going to do, the cut yet ripped open from the canine teeth. The laxatives that she had removed from her bosom were there beside her. She thought about it: Aunt Pip's bowels had moved only a little, her digestive system was breaking down.

She rose from the steps and called me to follow her into the kitchen to chop two blocks of laxatives on the counter of newspapers. The blade grated them into fine pieces, as I noticed, for the first time, the obituary that showed Big Mama's name, telling of how old she was, announcing to the women of Pyke County that a disease was going around, a disease of the breasts.

"We gotta open her up," said Fat.

Her flat feet rumbled through the house, stopping near the curtain draped over the window. "Pip," she whispered, "get up."

So calm was the response from Aunt Pip that she sounded cruel, beckoning for Fat to leave her alone. It was the atmosphere of effort. The living woman versus the dying one. Each arranging her vocabulary according to the price she had to pay for its use.

"Huh," said Aunt Pip, her breath pouring out of a deep sleep.

When I walked into the room, Fat was sitting behind her, pushing her upward from the back. You would have thought of violence at first, but she was rough this way. Her love was forced now, demanding.

"Give me the laxatives," said Fat.

Her hand, the bitten one, was outstretched, her arm balanced in the air with the resistance of an oar. Aunt Pip woke fully from her sleep and looked at her fingers, the diamond-shaped tear in the skin. Her eyes nursed the cut, wondering if it was only in her dreams that she envisioned this.

"Let me," I said.

Aunt Pip's arms were weak. She tried to fight me, but her energy did not allow it. Her head was turned now, facing the open window. The laxative was bitter in her mouth. She spat it out, and the pieces started to slide through her saliva. "I don't want it," she uttered. "Leave me be."

Fat stood up beside her and pushed her back on the pillows. Aunt Pip slid beneath the covers and fell asleep again. Her eyes reopened for a moment. She stared into the woods, the mother of the puppies still howling. "When I die," she said, reemerging, "take me to the center of the earth. Take me to the land of Eden."

She fell asleep upon her closed hands. Fat had walked to the screen door, her eyes following the trail of noises in the woods, the cut on her hand. Then, over to the mantel, wiping the dust from the photo of the two children. "All right," she said.

Moments later, the ax began to ricochet through the clouds again as I wiped the saliva from Aunt Pip's mouth, her face soft and quiet.

chapter
twenty-one

The sun was setting behind the moving clouds. All the windows were closed except for the breeze that came from Aunt Pip's curtain. She was sound asleep like the baby in my dream. Her face was turned inward, facing the direction of her breast. Her hands were overlapped, the elbows above her abdomen.

The blade of Fat's ax echoed through the trees. One chop and another and another. It was carefully guided. The object of focus, then the blade at the center of the already disturbed lumber.

I stood under the magnolia tree and looked back at the house where the curtains were beginning to settle down. The blade lost contact with the object, and I heard Fat's voice open up: "Dammit," she said.

I ran toward her and found her at the base of the oak tree breathing hard, the ax in her hands. Her legs were open and her panties were stained. Perhaps her tubes were emptying out their religion. My grandmother whispered to me one night, over a cold mountain of ice cubes in her lap: "Don't be bothered when your panties get dark," she'd say. "It's *Jesus* cleaning the devil out o' your stomach." Likewise, she had ignored the odor of her body, bathing herself in pine needles because she thought it drew the sickness out of her.

"Here!" yelled Fat. It took her a moment as she began to lift herself from the ground, forcing the ax on me. "You chop awhile. I chop awhile."

"What?"

"You heard me," she said, walking over to the steps of her house. "It's gotta come down sooner or later. I do what the good Lawd say do. Now get!"

The waist of the tree seemed as wide as the red sun behind her. Her arms were in her lap; her toes formed a pyramid in front of her.

"How you know it wasn't the devil?" I asked.

"'Cause I know the Lawd," she snapped.

I looked up at the widespread branches, how the limbs quivered in the pink-colored sky. A man had been hung there, hung like the hog at Mr. Jolie's, up high on a branch that cut the vein of life from his throat, the rope as sturdy and fixed as the penis of a rapist.

Fat's eyes were on the leaves of the tree. She got up from the steps and reached for one of the limbs, afterward coming back down on her heels because it was too high up to touch. She looked into the sky, the last cloud was clearing the earth. It grew imperfect, ordinary.

"You ever wonder why the 'h' in 'hour' is silent?" I asked.

She turned away from the limb. "Because it ain't no time."

"Then what we need it for?"

"It's a part of the world," she said, reaching for a tangled cobweb in front of her. "We got to be measured by something. If nothing controlled us, we wouldn't be afraid of death."

She took the cobweb and searched for unhatched eggs. When she found a cluster of them, she took her fingernail and slit them open. She thought that she had seen a baby. She sat the eggs on the ground and waited for the spiders to come out. "My panties get dark at night," she said.

"Maybe it's your period, Fat," I said.

I knew that it was not blood. I had seen Mama's panties after the yellow cream had filled them up, how she would wash them with bleach until the discharge turned gray and she could no longer be reminded of Daddy's need to push his fingers up a woman's stomach.

"No," said Fat, "I used to be clean as the Board of Health. I know what come from me. And it ain't no blood."

She was kneeling down now, watching the unhatched eggs for signs of life, activity. "When I was a little girl, Mama used to clean out my insides," she said. "She even took me to Jackson a couple o' times . . . even after I got grown and had my own place in New Orleans."

"What happened to her?"

Her eyes opened wide. She thought she had seen something: "She dead."

Fat seemed to grow tired of looking for life and began to plait her weak hair, one strand over another. "My daddy too." She paused, her thick fingers rewinding the one braid that seemed to crumble.

"I hated telling doctors what was wrong with me," she said. "Men like to tell you how much you ain't perfect."

I remembered my grandma's words, how she told me about the man in the white coat, how he had made her uncomfortable and that she was too afraid to tell him his fingers were in the wrong place, cutting the wrong part of her. This is what killed her babies to come: embarrassment.

I stepped away from the tree. "Want me to help you?"

A faint smile came over Fat's face. Her fingers fell from the last braid, and she relaxed them on her stomach. "You can't wash out a killing," she said. "When you get grown, get saved. 'Cause the end come quick. And it ain't a matter of time and clocks no more. You be dead."

She did not look uncomfortable. Her skin was spotless now, the eyebrows emerging into a shadow over her eyes. She walked toward Aunt Pip's house. "Let's go," she said. "Pip be waiting."

chapter
twenty-two

The windows and doors were open. I was in a place with no calendars. Everything I had endured was somehow seeping upon me, and the mothers and grandmothers and daughters of breast cancer were gathering themselves around me, circling the wooden floor that housed my naked body.

It was no dream now.

A long vertical mirror reflected the shame that I felt for having a full head of hair, eyebrows, two growing breasts, nipples— all the elements that Aunt Pip herself had been through. I looked upon her. The breeze from the windows flaring against her breastbone where half of her fat was missing. I removed the covers from her pelvis and lay beside her, feeling where the bones connected in the encyclopedia, those I had studied many times when I wondered where the alcohol of my father's body was going. Her own bones had grown brittle and timid. I lay there upon the last nipple, sucking it as the curtains flared away from us. Her small hands enclosed me.

"My milk is gone," she said.

I took her lips in my hands and kissed them. "Sleep," I said before walking back into the bathroom and sharpening a razor that had been sitting there on the porcelain face bowl, flat. The shutters of the house tapped. Rain was forming in the clouds. A sudden howling of thunder echoed over Pyke County, past my house and other houses of bastards and backsliders like Diamond and past Fat's place, where she was somewhere waiting for Aunt Pip to wither away completely.

I pressed the razor against my scalp. The hairs of my head were falling down over my shoulders. No man would rape me because of it. No cancer would enter my breasts and take my voice, nothing left for the doctors to rid me of. Or put the lumps from my body in glass jars like the flesh of Willie's brain.

Piles and piles of hair landed on the floor.

Now I was plucking the hairs of my vagina. The white bulbs at the base of them were circular. With each strand of hair, a pain echoed through my abdomen. And the women and grandmothers and daughters of breast cancer danced around me: their eyebrows gone and their breasts gone and their scalps bare, dancing with tears coming down upon their bareness.

A mother, both breasts missing, stood behind her daughter. She grabbed hold of other daughters and grandmothers as they picked me up and swung me into the dance. They danced until the thunder came down and the rain. God had begun to cry. But it wasn't because we had upset Him: they had blessed the earth.

They wanted to show me the center. I ran with them, through the front door, until I could no longer feel my footsteps. I saw all things: the tiniest cricket being born, an ant standing on all fours as the rain fell upon it, the unfolding of the magnolias, no longer dead but alive, Fat crying inside her hands, Aunt Pip lying on the mattress with her vertebrae stitching itself back into the muscle, erected.

Beautiful women they were. They smiled and took my hands in their hands. The rain came down on us as the blues darkened and turned into charcoal. They took me there to the center. As we approached, I found myself running alone into the forest, falling hard onto the ground. The journey weakened me. The experience weakened me.

There was a hole there. Landy Collins had measured it perfectly. I knew that when I had seen him talking to Mama, he was taking down Aunt Pip's measurements: the weight of her body upon death, the length of her shoulders, as he had done Willie.

I was as Fat had been: I had stopped looking at him as help. But instead, as a man.

And he was not in the business of pleasure. He was a casket maker, a carpenter of death. I, among others, was his Eve, and he was the man who had written my name down in the books of young girls, fools.

The hole was deep. I crawled over the edge of it and waited for the lightning to come down. My nude body flattened against the earth as if I had been born from that same center.

Lightning struck. Before I could see any farther into the hole, I noticed a young flower slowly being swallowed by the rainwater. It floated atop the surface of the hole, way down deep where the roots were unnoticeable. It hadn't completely sprouted but was still green and managed to keep its head just above the rising water.

As I looked out into the forest, I saw a woman's eyes. Only a woman's eyes could glow like that. She was not a part of the others, the other women who had flung me to the ground with their energy. Her eyes were even deeper.

The lightning struck again, and there at my feet was a wooden coffin, sacredly positioned across from the hole, noticeable.

I heard footsteps again.

When death is near, any sound will do. Something to grab your attention besides the deep, tranquilized breathing, the whistling of wilted magnolias, the ax of a woman who believed that God's voice had come to her in the middle of the night, telling her to chop down what was already dead. Because the blood of a hanging had rotted it from the inside out.

"Who's there?" I asked, listening to the footsteps leave the forest.

I walked over to the coffin and opened the lid. The mud of the forest saturated the earth as I ran my fingers along the edge of the coffin, a death basket soon to be filled by a disease, a woman soon to die in a woman's way. That bald head of hers fitting perfectly into the skull part of the coffin where every sin that she'd committed went down with her. The bones sinking into the pine and creating a stir for the undergrounders, those who must be buried because the flesh had an odor to it. Landy had built it perfectly. A perfect coffin. I lay down inside it with my back against the bed of it, closing the lid. I lay there thinking of how I was the blessed one. How many of the living had the chance to lie where the dead must lie? How many would choose to?

"We must listen to the dead," my grandmother always told me. "Listen to them. They have a story to tell. You will never be where they are unless God changes time and time changes Him." She'd sit up with the sun shining down on her. "And that will never happen."

The footsteps were reemerging in the forest.

I opened the lid of the coffin. "Who are you?" I asked.

She said nothing. Suddenly, I saw her eyes again. They were heavenly. The glow from them was too bright for a dark world. "Who are you?" I asked again. "Say something."

As the women had not been a dream, neither were the eyes of this woman. I crawled out of the coffin and closed the lid. As I walked through the woods, the eyes disappeared. Who was she? Where did she come from? "Wait!" I yelled.

She turned around once more and walked clear out of sight.

I ran back to the house. When I opened the door, Aunt Pip was sitting in the dark.

"Where have you been?" she whispered.

The moon exposed my nude body. "The forest."

She turned without saying a word about my flesh: "*Jesus.*"

I went to the bathroom and slid a gown over my body. My heart had begun to pound as I felt the women going back into the sky where their bodies turned into stars.

"Maddy," said Aunt Pip, "I need you. Come lay next to me."

Before I made it to her, she broke down on the pillows, crying so loudly that the love in my heart hurt as it had when I had stood behind her at the piano. "Don't cry," I said, taking her head in my bosom. When the light lit up my scalp, she looked at me in the strangest way.

"Christ be the glory," she said as I took her hand and ran it across my head.

"This is your love," I said.

She cried so pitifully. Cancer inside a woman's body was a caterpillar, green like the caterpillars of a naked woman who bathed outside in the nude, green like Mama's hands. Aunt Pip was the dead. As much as I loved her and hated for her to die, she was the dead.

"My milk is gone," she whispered. "I swallowed my Father and now I'm paying for it."

I held her. "You'll get it back someday."

The white of her eyes glowed through the darkness. "Go," she said, trying to push me away from her. "Get one o' them mason jars out of the kitchen. Tell Fat to put me some milk in there."

"Don't talk like that," I said.

"Fat's got all that milk," she said. "She can afford to. Fat's a big girl. She's top-heavy. Tell her to squeeze herself up and bring me some o' that fine milk God gave her."

I peeled her hands from my skin. "I can't do that, Aunt Pip," I said. "Please."

She grew quiet. She looked at me as if she had never seen me before. Death was on her. She knew that death was on her as much as the fear in a hog's eyes when it knows that a man stands behind it with a knife in his hands—to kill it.

"I ain't nothing without my milk," said Aunt Pip.

She paused in her agony and held me while God sent thunder and lightning through the clouds. I lay there thinking about the forest and the coffin and the woman's eyes guiding her into the forest where I could no longer see her tiny shoulders curving outward from the pine.

chapter
twenty-three

Several days later, I woke to find the empty mason jar from my house sitting on the front porch. Mama had been there, quietly guiding her footsteps on the boards, just below the window. She had been there, indeed, her body carrying the scent of juniper, arousing the balance of wind behind her.

Aunt Pip was no longer eating. In the morning hours, I removed the covers from her legs and oiled them. Her skin was becoming dry, cracked. And her mouth was always covered in a white line of foam. She was dehydrated. I dipped my fingers into a water-filled cup and let the fluid drip into her mouth, turning her head in the direction of the ceiling for it to flow down her throat.

The air began to penetrate the room. You cannot imagine the silence. Not even a barking dog with rabies to pierce the clouds, no tractors or white men in the green field beside us, the propellers of a faraway plane in the sky. Nothing. Just the rotation of an antique fan sending its wind upon the covers.

I lay down on the floor next to her bed, waiting for the moment when she would turn around to scold me or demand for her urine to be dumped. Something. The movement of an arm, a foot, her swatting a buzzing fly from her ear with a fragile hand.

Cancer had come into Aunt Pip's house and taken it over. Everything was cancerous: the roof, the walls, the kitchen sink, the piano. Everything inside of her house. And no human born of any character known was strong enough to witness it and not have it touch them somewhere deep down inside. Deep where the faces of disease go and hide from the flesh. A place where the dead go and leave the living to their deaths.

I knocked on Fat's door.

"What is it?" she asked.

She looked into my eyes and turned away. Never minding my bald head, she started for the bedroom. The walls were so thin. She fumbled around a little while before her fat broke onto the bed. She cried and cried and told God to get out of her house if He couldn't stay: "You bring life in here," she said. "But you always take it away."

She lay on the wooden bed, holding on to the sides of the mattress as if nothing in her life had been pleasing. As she closed her eyes, a tear rolled down the side of her face. "You always think you can do it till the last days come." She held up her fists and shook them like God was in the room but wasn't listening to her.

"I know I shouldn't be mad at Pip," she said, "but I am. I told her about all that running around and wearing them thin clothes in the wintertime."

She rocked herself back and forth on the bed. The pattern of her thoughts depended on how much the bed squeaked from the weight of her body. She'd mumble something, then stop. Mumble, then stop. The bed squeaked. The louder the bed, the louder she'd become. "Lawd," she said, getting on her knees and pulling me down with her, "please don't take my Pip. I always tol' you that if anybody went first, let it be me. Not Pip. Please don't take my Pip, Lawd."

The hole in her mouth grew wider as she walked over to the window and looked at her work: the ax was still in the tree. She then went over to a wooden drawer and pulled out an envelope. Her hands were touching the surface of it now, and when she laid it down, I saw the numbers in the upper left-hand corner and the four letters that I would never forget: MDOC.

A storm was brewing in the clouds. There was no thunder or lightning. The sky was the color of a wild mushroom, drifting over Pyke County in growing darkness.

Aunt Pip was in a coma now. Her muscles were relaxed, her arms and legs limp from dehydration, no food. Fat ran some hot water into the metal bedpan after thoroughly cleansing it of urine with vinegar and lye soap. She sat at the foot of the mattress with Aunt Pip's legs in her lap, holding them up and scrubbing the bed dust from them. Fat was not as rough as she once was. Something had changed her, an odd occurrence of magnetism. Her eyes were drawn to a distant corner of the room, listening to the pace of her breathing in the silence.

I was at the head of the bed, holding Aunt Pip's face in my lap. Her skin was warm. I lightly touched the bone that had been pressed against the kitchen window, the lower jaw connecting with the upper, the sharp teeth placed vertically together. Inside her mouth lived a tongue that would no longer be used. There would be no more of her birdlike voice, emerging from her stomach to say something, anything, that made her upset. Nothing of her lying on her back on the wooden boards of the porch to reach for the darkness behind her. Or the quiet laughter that erupted after Fat had blown a line of smoke up her nose.

"Look at her," said Fat, rubbing the bottom of Aunt Pip's feet with oil now.

She looked at her intimately. Two women who had carried each other through the rumors. An adulteress and the widow of a hanged man. Their language was hidden beyond the house walls, their secrets, the unknown photo of the children playing in the face of a rubber hosepipe.

Fat stood up from the mattress; the thumping of her feet was heard in the kitchen, stopping at the window. Her hand was on her chest now, pounding beneath her blouse to keep herself from crying. It did not work for when the pounding stopped, she broke out into a stream of tears.

"Lawd," she whispered, "I ain't got nothing or nobody. My folks got burnt out. My chiren gone." She was no longer shouting out her words. "I know I ain't got no business being mad at the sick. But I just can't help it."

She mumbled, then stopped. The patting continued.

Why couldn't death have been as simple as pulling the yellow strand of hair from Mama's forehead? What did God do with the missing breasts of women? Did the doctors keep them in a room of radioactive machines to study it, one woman's disease after another? I was on my feet. My legs were weak beneath me. I lifted my arm and studied my own growing breast, just like Mama had done. I couldn't afford to lie down the way the models had done in the books. Because I knew that a lump was a lump. It did not matter if I was comfortable enough to feel it. Anything inside of my body that wasn't supposed to be there would show itself to me; it would throw me off balance, eat me.

There was nothing there. Only flesh.

And when I turned to cover Aunt Pip's body, I noticed a moving muscle beneath the covers, traveling up toward her middle part. My hand crawled on the bone of Aunt Pip's leg. She had lost weight rapidly. It was different to see what the cancer had done, but to touch it. The face was already a perfect thing. What could a woman's face lose that wasn't there in the beginning? The face was designed in the stomach, the pulse of the abdomen vibrating in its chain-saw rhythm, chiseling the skull into a triangle, a pyramid, a coffin. But this I had missed altogether. Nothing is solid except the moment a child notices, through some odd event, that what she had failed to recognize was what she was destined to become.

There, upon the map of my hand, was the green lizard from the mason jar. I touched it and brought it close to me. Mama had been there over the window, quietly sitting the mason jar on the porch, reaching inside the open window to lift the covers from Aunt Pip's abdomen. And there it was, the lizard that had been there all the while since, lying in wait, hiding beneath the covers for the breath to leave Aunt Pip's body.

I let it go. And it crawled back to her abdomen, its tail curled lazily on the tip of her vagina.

chapter
twenty-four

Fat was in the kitchen picking up private things when the gravity of the porcelain doll pulled me to it. Nothing was happening slowly anymore. I stood near the mantel, listening to the howling of the mad animal.

The doll sat next to the record player, her body chipped down the center, the fractured hole in her ribs exposed. I stuck my finger down her throat and felt the coldness of something. I pulled it out of her mouth.

It was a photo of my birth.

There, with her legs open, was Mama, the blood of her vagina filled the towels, her large breasts hanging beside her. Nothing in the room was white. And I could not see Mama's face. But I knew, as all children knew, the vaginas they came from: the manner in which the fur rests between the muscles of their thighs, the battered stillness of their lungs upon birth. Beside Mama was Aunt Pip, holding me as I sucked the milk from her breast.

And through the silence, my grandmother spoke to me: You was caught in the tubes.

Now I knew why Mama had opened my mouth and pinned down the muscle in my throat. Aunt Pip had pulled me out of her stomach. And like my grandmother, she could not lie next to me in the days to come because the smell of death was yet on my body. I was the baby in my dreams—the blood from the tubes of my mother's stomach suffocating me like a green lizard trapped in the space of a mason jar. I was a part of the world now. The milk of a whore's breast was in my mouth, and I needed to see, for my own mother's sake, the wrath that God had put upon a mistress. Because she had prayed for the saved breast, not the unsaved one, never knowing that I would soon be old enough to smell the milk of Aunt Pip's breast on a tube of fire-engine-red lipstick—that which she had lain on a flat bed of porcelain, the words of *Jesus* calling me to it.

This was the way that it was in the beginning.

Because blood and milk are the same.

A set of headlights was headed toward the house. Fat was now reading the red letters of the Bible, the ones that came from *Jesus*. She told me that they were most important. The others didn't count because they were not the voice of Christ.

"Lawdy mercy," she said. "Who that be at this hour?"

The car stopped in front of the house. The dying motor sounded familiar. With the headlights still on, a man emerged, taking off his hat on the steps, pausing. He looked over at the lantern, the stillness of it, how private and solitary it was along the porch. The man was Willie's grandfather, the deacon.

Fat met him at the door, taking his hat: "Thank God," she said.

The lonely howling of the rabid dog was in the woods. It had not rained. The clouds managed to pass over Pyke County going eastward. But the fear of the night, it had left behind.

His mouth was closed. A moment passed through his lips. He looked at me with some sort of pity. Or power, perhaps. A bead of sweat trickled down his throat. And when he touched my hand, the dog stopped her howling.

"Lemme take your jacket, Deacon," said Fat.

He shook his head at first. Then, after seeing Aunt Pip asleep on the bed, the covers pulled down to her waist, the darkness of her face, he changed his mind. "Mighty welcome," he said.

There was a hole in his shirt the size of an avocado. It went up from the side of his stomach to the edge of his ribs, the part in the encyclopedia that turned into the sharp tip of a kitchen knife. He put his fingers over Aunt Pip's private part, back to her breast, the private part again, the empty part of her chest that the doctors had stitched into a scorpion. "Let us pray," he said.

"Lawd," he said, "we come to you in prayer." He began to pull the thin layer of skin between his eyes. "The flesh is tired, Father. I don't doubt that it's weak. It's always been that way. But now it's tired." He patted his knee. "I come to you in no time or place," he said. "For I don't have the power to give you the hour of a heavy soul. We on borrowed time. How we live is how we die."

Neither Fat nor I could hold back the tears. The blades of a fan had been our sole company. When neither of us could speak, the cold silence of the room around us, we listened to the rotating wind float throughout the house, hoping that somewhere in the midst of the noise, the coma would take Aunt Pip to the other side. But she was fighting, even on her deathbed: a light twitch of her eyes, a quick moment of her chest rising to interrupt her normal breathing pattern, a path of chills on the surface of her arm.

The deacon's hand rested on the scar of Aunt Pip's missing breast. He prayed and prayed over that hole until the Holy Ghost caught him. The wind began to pick up the avocado-sized patch in his shirt. "Yes, Lawd Almighty," he said. "The soul is naked. Take it! Have your way with it, Lawd!

"The only time you should look down on somebody is when you picking them up," said the deacon.

And were my eyes not witnessing the hole in his shirt, I would have missed it altogether. There it was, a shining scar with the familiarity of a missing kidney, because it slept inside a white man's body, a postman, and healed him.

"Amen," he said, bringing himself to his feet and closing the jacket in about him.

chapter
twenty-five

I lay there on the pallet, the yellow moon broken up into jagged pieces on the floor. Above my body, on the mantel, was a glass of water; the balance of it was an inch away from the rim. It was a transparent object, nothing clouding it except the fingerprints of a human hand.

When you are in darkness, your fingers and mind search for things that are not there, things that you feel you are somehow responsible for. But I knew for sure that I had heard the early beginnings of footsteps. The exact ones that walked through the forest the night before the doctors took Aunt Pip's hair.

One . . . two . . . and the third dropping off. It was not a constant sound or activity. It was more like the creature had stopped to look around, underneath the yellow light of the moon, for security. One . . . two . . . and before the third was heard, the footsteps began to fade away.

Fat stood over me, her hands on her large hips. Had her arms been outstretched, she could have been Jesus Christ. "Pip," she said, her voice breaking the silence of the room, "we going to New Orleans."

I was in the right place to pray, on the floor, with the glass of water over my head, hoping that it would lose its balance and baptize me.

"Let's bathe her," said Fat. "Go run some water."

Before anything else, I went out the back door and grabbed an armful of pine needles. Aunt Pip couldn't talk to me now. She couldn't tell me what she wanted.

Fat had begun to talk to herself: "I'm gonna bathe my Pip."

The last time she'd been alone with death was when Justice died. Those white men hanged him from the oak tree and took his heart. They killed him and left his flesh to rot where the oak tree had claimed her house and made her sore.

I filled the tub with hot water. The pine needles floated to the top. Everything came to a head: the sound of the stove lighting up for a bowl of soup, the doe, *Jesus,* Laurel Pillar, the pills, Mama, death.

"I need help in here, Maddy," yelled Fat.

I rolled the covers back from Aunt Pip's neck. Her bones felt like a child had traced them out on a piece of paper and toted them to school underneath his arm. Thin like that. Thin enough to be drawn out on a sheet of loose-leaf paper and delivered.

"My God," said Fat, looking at Aunt Pip's body. "What they do to my baby?"

The footsteps picked up again.

"Do you hear that?" asked Fat. "We going home."

Aunt Pip's feet were so very warm in my hands. That's where the good blood was. She had carried a fever in the lowest part of her body. They were pointed. I tried several times to bend them, but her fight against death was strongest where her feet had flattened out the muscles in her fingertips. "I got her," I said. "Let's go."

Fat lit three candles and fixed them around the bathroom: over the window, in the sink below the mirror, on the shoulder of the porcelain bathtub. We moved the pine straw out of the way. Aunt Pip's arm hung lifelessly: over and over again, Fat pulled her body up from the water and cried over the scar. "Maddy," she said, "what they do to my Pip?"

She stood up from the bathtub with her back to me. She was peeling the clothes from her body now, heading for New Orleans, where they had both laughed with men who did not deserve them, walked the streets with their arms closed tightly around each other. The loaves of fat hung from her abdomen. And when she lifted her arms above her head, the fat rose a little, to complement the change in her body. A bear had not been the right word to describe her. She was made of lead, solidly written upon the green slate of the earth like Moses and the Ten Commandments fingered into stone with the hand of wisdom.

"Lawd, Pip," she said, pulling back the mirror above the sink. There it was, the kerosene-filled bottle. She looked at it, her hand opening the small cap, smelling it: "Get me the lantern."

"I'm scared, Fat."

The tears fell. "Don't be scared," she said. "Let Him use you."

Somewhere on the other side of town, my mother's birthmark was turning red. She was going through the house moving furniture and lighting candles. She didn't have the words, the strength to come. But she knew that death was in this house tonight. She and Aunt Pip were of the same womb. No matter what room of the house Mama was in, it was eating her alive that she couldn't come to Commitment Road and listen to the dead.

The lantern sat on the porch. The mud of the earth was still on it. How it felt inside my hands: the curved body, the long, narrow wire pressed against the palm of my flesh. I was grateful, for there was someone in the world, like Aunt Pip, like Willie, who could not feel this intimacy, this connection with a living thing.

I returned to the bathroom with the lantern; Fat was holding Aunt Pip, her hand over the scar in her chest. "Sit it down," she said.

The footsteps picked up again. They were in threes now. Not even in Mama's counting did I hear the third step, the Holy Ghost. "Listen," said Fat, closing her eyes.

She said this innocently. There was a time when a diseased woman lay on the boards of the house with me and did not hear the sound of these footsteps.

Fat put her hand on Aunt Pip's still-beating heart and said: "They coming for us. I hear them."

The women were surrounding us now: Aunt Pip's life was in their hands. They were warming the blood in her body and loving her feet and hands. Fat heard them. They were in the mirrors of the house, on the doorsteps, in the piano room, singing and holding their missing breasts with living hands.

"Where is it?" asked Fat, pulling Aunt Pip up by the waist, her arms draped over her thick shoulders.

"What?"

"The lipstick."

The fire-engine-red lipstick was yet inside the brown paper bag that Fat'd brought the first time I saw her. There it was on the shelf, next to all the things that the living used: the baking soda, toothpaste, baby powder. "Here," I said.

"Hold her head up," said Fat as I sat behind her on the toilet.

I did. Fat leaned over and put Aunt Pip's face inside her hands, kissing her lips before spreading a thin layer of the lipstick on them. She grew silent. The dog that had bitten her finger was howling in the darkness. She occasionally looked up to listen for the women and their voices.

"Pip," she said, "I love you."

The tears came down. There was no sound at all. Fat kissed Aunt Pip's lips while holding the red inside her hands: "Amen," she said.

I flattened my face against Aunt Pip's backbone. The grooves in her spine went through my flesh, and I felt their sharpness on the bridge of my missing wisdoms. You must hold the dead in their last days. Look into their eyes and listen to their voices. The dying know not what you do for them. They live in the spirit. They can no longer speak your language. Your words mean nothing to their bones. It is their spirit that listens.

Fat turned around and opened the baby powder. The holes of air were blocked. When she blew over the top of them, the white powder rose into a white cloud above us. "No one will ever take your fur again," she said.

She stepped back and looked over what she had done. She was in another world. I did not know where she was. It was far beyond me. I was still green. Green like the land of Eden where the flesh was confused, where green was so beautiful that nobody noticed it. Because mankind had opened their mouths and eaten it. We had all swallowed our Father. We ate of a measured place where our lives were limited and unbalanced in human understanding. Not knowing that there was no understanding in human language. Only greenness and death.

Fat left the bathroom and came back with Aunt Pip's blond wig. I lifted Aunt Pip's chin and waited for her to put it on her head. "We going to New Orleans," said Fat, laughing and holding herself at the stomach. "Remember, Pip?" she asked. "Everybody wanted us." She stiffened her shoulders. "They all wanted us."

Aunt Pip began to wheeze. I felt the sickness coming up through her spine and letting her go. Not saving her. Just letting her go. There was a moment when the spirit overpowered the sickness.

The sickness could no longer hang on. It had fucked up the body. The body was temporary, but the spirit went to a place where disease had no place. It turned around at the gates of heaven and slumped its shoulders, detached itself from the green, from Eden.

We made our way to the bed, where we laid her nudeness down on the bed she had been in. Her old abandoned gown hung on the front porch for the night wind to carry away. "Cover her up," said Fat.

I put my hands underneath the white quilt again, moving along the fabric in search of the green lizard. I found it. This thing itself was dying. The spirit of Daddy's hand was still around it, strangling it from the eye of the kitchen window.

It fit so neatly inside the white handkerchief, its body wrapped, covered. I had no memory of how the fabric had gotten into my hands. When the living are dying, there is but one thought that takes over all others: death.

"Me and Pip's going to New Orleans."

I could not remember the hour, the minutes, the seconds of which we coated Aunt Pip's hands and feet with oil again. But I do remember sliding the lizard over her abdomen, letting it go. Aunt Pip lay there with her arms beside her and the covers coming up every now and then when her breathing became too unbearable.

"Let us pray," said Fat, kneeling beside the bed. "Lawd, me and Pip's going to New Orleans. Watch over us and feed us on our journey. Take us home, Lawd. Bury us there. Leave us." She lifted her breasts in her hands. "Take us to where men call us by our first names," she said. "Amen and amen."

Beside her lay the glass lantern. She picked it up as she peeled the quilt back from Aunt Pip's face and smiled. "Ain't nobody gonna take my Pip 'way from me now."

The footsteps were louder now.

The women were out there in the forest, leading us back to where Landy Collins had dug the hole. Barefoot and naked, Fat held Aunt Pip's body in her arms; the glass lantern dangled from her hand. We started for the forest. The creatures of the world were asleep. No crickets chirping or the sound of blowflies on a piece of sliced cantaloupe. If I had not been in darkness, I would have known nothing of light or creatures or the noise of living things.

We heard something.

Fat stopped to look down at her feet. We both knew what it was now; a stream of urine had come from Aunt Pip's bladder: she was dead.

Every tear that I had been holding back came out. They flowed through me from my stomach; they became my voice. Everything lived in darkness. *Jesus* put our pain in the dark so we'd pay more attention to our eyes, our noses, our hands, our flesh, the part of us that we failed to witness, because the beauty of its being was what blinded us. He blessed us and blessed us until we walked in our own darknesses.

Fat laid Aunt Pip's body beside the hole and looked into the mouth of the glass lantern. The moon was no longer yellow but blue. And with this light, Fat took the match from the lantern and struck it on the base. There it was! A flame that ignited the up-turned wick. I could not see the faces of the women. I did not know them, only their missing parts. And the cancer that had eaten away at them.

Fat moved her fingers over the scar as the deacon had done, letting out a loud noise. She then opened the lid of the coffin. "We gots to be going now," she said. "Walk away."

"But Fat . . ." I said.

"Don't cry for us," she said. "We going to New Orleans!"

At that moment, the oak tree that she had been chopping on for so many days came crashing down, as if it had become weak at the waist. With its noise, she closed her eyes and sighed, her nude body collapsing to the earth. "Go," she said.

It was then that she began to sing:

> *It won't be water*
> *But fire next time*

I ran for a short while before looking back to find her hovering over Aunt Pip's coffin. There, circling them both, was the bearer of footsteps: the naked lady whom I had drawn on the first page of Genesis, her chest as flat as a man's, her face blank and clear, beautiful. Fat looked at her and smiled. The glass lantern was high over her head now, her hands around its throat. She looked at me in the distance and simply let it fall into the hole, setting off the burning kerosene, before jumping into the rising flames.

I ran back to the house to find Mama standing on the front porch with her hands in the air. The miles of Deuteronomy had been beaten into her. The closer I grew toward her, she knew that Aunt Pip was gone. "No!" she yelled. "My God, no.

"This is my home," she said. "I left my heart here."

But it was too late.

She was already dead.

epilogue

Here, lying open-eyed on the pallet beside Aunt Pip's bed, I recalled the shadow that had awakened me the night before I discovered the mason jar on the front porch. It was a man's footsteps, his hesitant pattern of breathing, his one arm on the windowsill. It was my father.

Somewhere in the midst of his nudity, he was changing. He was well aware of his past, the use of his fingers going up the hole of a woman's vagina. He remembered the last image of his brother being pulled away from the tubular glass, into the arms of a guard, back into the jail cell with the other numbers. Nothing happens by accident. It was no coincidence that he had burnt down the factory of Jesus, the man whom he'd blamed for the course of his diseased life. He had not listened, as I had, to the pastor when he said that *Jesus* was of the spirit. But because he had found a man with the same name, the man he had given his life to, it was easier to distort the physical. The physical could be found like the embalmed kings of worshiped men in other countries, their followers who consider it tangible to believe in what they can see. Not in what they cannot see. It was no act of circumstance that my father had found himself in the shoes of the raped, the sick woman with only one breast to touch. It was his shadow, indeed, reminiscing, hoping to correct the wrongs of his past, so that all things in death could be accounted for through repentance. So that he would now know what it felt like to have something hurt him. Something God made.

The rabid dog barked in the distance, her howling now dying off in the woods of the forest. How much longer did she have to live? What would happen to her? The road was blue now. She was out there watching the flames, the bodies, the breastless spirit dance around the pyre.

The things that shaped my thoughts: Aunt Pip had returned to a life of diapers like babies at birth. For babies know nothing of the world they are born into. They are brought forth by images, women with no names or faces. I was thinking of the letter I'd found hidden in the jewelry box beneath Aunt Pip's bed, the letter she had written to *Jesus* because she had wanted him to change her sister's heart, only to have it returned by the Bible company she had addressed it to, telling her that they were in the business of publishing God's Word and whosoever shall find the Word shall keep it. This was the mumbling that she'd committed herself to all those nights when I was deaf and could not listen, because I was lost in the rattles of distant things.

I was lost in the land of Eden.

acknowledgments

My sisters and brothers for coming together when they used to: Renee, Dana, Ricky, Ollie, Landy, and Cheryl. My nieces and nephews: Jacque, Cortney, Blake, Billy, Nature, Tre, Darion, Jasmine, and Oliver's family. Aunt Seleria Jones for the inspiration.

Thomas Williams for the ink cartridges, the reams of paper, the coffee, and for adopting me from the hand of God.

My second mother, Carole McAllister, for feeding me the many years that I probably would have starved to death, for keeping the light in my eyes. No one of flesh will ever know how much I suffered more than you. Judy Kahn for feeling my commitment to words. And Alba Taylor: fight!

My friends who knew that I was empty and never mentioned my poverty: Cathy Pope, Fredric Fland, Gary Smith, Geoffrey Ball, Cedric Dangerfield, Johari Ellis, Brett Eames, Bryce Williams.

The following professors: William Dowie, Jim Bennett (the first to read *Eden*), Joe Kronick, Andrei Codrescu, my pal, and Rick

Blackwood. Moira Crone, for introducing me to my agent, Amy Williams (my verbal firecracker!).

Special thanks to Lauren for the special notes attached to the samples and her efforts to shake the tail of a dragon with loose fingers. And my editor, Elisabeth, who sorted through the character trees and symbols to find the gem. Thank you to the first to allow me to put my dream down on pages and for truly getting it— to the hippest team of the publishing world, Grove/Atlantic.

To the late: Geraldine Cimino, Aunt Barbara Ann, Cathy Kagle, Thelma McAllister, Annie Lee Hurst, Alice Reams, Gwen Porter, Evelyn Blackmor Skaggs, Aunt Creola Vemon-Batchelor, and the baby that was lost in my mama's stomach.

Lastly, Mama for bringing me into the world with a pen in my hand.

I wish I could thank you all. There is not enough space in the world.